The Ho

THE M... OF THE WIDOW'S WATCH

John Bibee

InterVarsity Press
Downers Grove, Illinois

InterVarsity Press® is the book-publishing division of InterVarsity Christian Fellowship/USA®, a student movement active on campus at hundreds of universities, colleges and schools of nursing in the United States of America, and a member movement of the International Fellowship of Evangelical Students. For information about local and regional activities, write Public Relations Dept., InterVarsity Christian Fellowship/USA, 6400 Schroeder Rd., P.O. Box 7895, Madison, WI 53707-7895.

Cover illustration: David Darrow

ISBN 0-8308-1918-5

Printed in the United States of America 

Library of Congress Cataloging-in-Publication Data

Bibee, John.
The mystery of the widow's watch / John Bibee.
p. cm. — (The Home School Detectives ; 8)
Summary: When the Home School Dectectives respond to an old woman's plea to help her find her dead husband's missing gold watch, they discover some mysterious activities at the nursing home where she lives.
ISBN 0-8308-1918-5 (pbk.)
[1. Nursing homes—Fiction. 2. Christian life—Fiction. 3. Mystery and detective stories.] I. Title. II. Series: Bibee, John. Home School Detectives ; 8.
PZ7.B471465Myw 1998
[Fic]—dc21 *98-21210*
CIP
AC

---

15 14 13 12 11 10 9 8 7 6 5 4 3 2 1
08 07 06 05 04 03 02 01 00 99 98

Chapter One

Mrs. Babbage's Urgent Question

"Mrs. Babbage sounded real upset this morning when she talked to me," Julie said to Rebecca and Emily. The three friends were in Julie's room just before nine o'clock on Saturday morning. Julie Brown had just finished brushing her dog, Toby, a golden Labrador retriever. Toby wagged his tail and ran out of the room.

"Who's next?" Julie held the dog brush up, as if inviting the others.

"Not me," Rebecca Renner laughed.

"Me neither," Emily Morgan said. "I was groomed yesterday. But to get back to the subject, why do you think Mrs. Babbage was upset?"

"I couldn't tell why, but you could hear it in her voice,"

Julie said. "She's called three times already. She left two messages on the answering machine, and then before I could call her back, she called again, just before you all got here. She keeps saying she'll pay us even though I told her that wasn't necessary. She's read about our detective work in the newspapers."

"I think we should try to help her," Rebecca said with a determined look on her face. "We're going to the Manor House anyway. She didn't say what she wanted us to do?"

"No, and that was kind of the odd part," Julie replied. "She said she didn't want to talk over the phone. She also said she was tired because she'd been up most of the night. One of the residents at the Manor House, Mr. Binton, had a heart attack and died last night. There was a big commotion. Mrs. Babbage said she hardly slept."

"That must have been why she was upset," Rebecca said.

"Maybe . . ." Julie replied uncertainly. "I didn't sleep very well last night. I had a really strange dream. I was being chased, and it was real scary."

"I hate being chased in dreams," Rebecca said.

Emily's forehead wrinkled in a frown. She didn't seem to be listening to the others. "Mrs. Babbage seems a little senile to me. I'm not trying to be unkind, but you know how some people get. My grandmother Morgan has Alzheimer's disease, and she is really forgetful and confused. The last time I was there, she thought I was my mother's sister, my aunt Mary. She kept calling me Mary and asking me questions that didn't make sense."

"Really?" Rebecca asked. "Do you look like your aunt when she was your age?"

"Not a bit, according to my mother," Emily said. "Aunt

Mary always had short dark hair. And our faces aren't anything alike. My grandmother was just really confused. It's sad because she used to be really different. She used to be a librarian and really smart and knew all kinds of things. Now she can't even tie her shoes. It's hard to believe someone can change so much in such a short time. My mother almost always cries after we visit her."

"That's sad," Julie agreed, frowning. "Your grandmother is younger than my grandparents. They are pretty healthy. They live in their own homes."

"I hope no one in my family ever gets that sick," Rebecca whispered. "My Pop-Pop had skin cancer, but he got better. If I get sick, I just hope it doesn't hurt too much. But I'd really hate it if I got all confused and crazy. At least I think I would. Does your grandmother know she is confused?"

"We're not really sure what she knows or how she thinks," Emily said.

"Well, I don't think Mrs. Babbage has Alzheimer's," Julie said. "She is quite old. We can ask her what she wants us to investigate. But if it sounds too wacky or weird—"

"We can tell her we're busy," Rebecca said.

"We don't have to lie," Julie said. "We can just say something like we don't think we can help her."

"Uh-oh, Mrs. Smoot just drove up," Becky said. "And Clarice is with her too."

"Really?" Emily said. "I thought she wouldn't come this time. She hates going to the Manor House."

"My mom said she wants us to be extra nice to her," Julie replied glumly. "I got a big lecture this morning at breakfast. I told my mom what Clarice said at the church youth group last week about us. My mom said we need to be forgiving. That mistakes happen."

"But Clarice never even said she was sorry," Rebecca protested. "She practically calls us thieves, and then she finds her CD player the next day in the trunk of her dad's car. We wouldn't even have known except that her brother told us the truth."

"That's what I told my mom," Julie replied. "But she said we 'need to keep the door open' so Clarice can apologize. She says that since the Smoots have only lived in Springdale a few months, it may take a while to get to know Clarice and 'appreciate all her qualities,' to quote my mom. She also said Mrs. Smoot is worried because Clarice doesn't have many friends at her school and doesn't fit in easily."

"There are probably good reasons for that," Rebecca said dryly.

"I told my mom that, but she says we need to be good examples anyway," Julie fumed. "If I get told to be a good example one more time this morning, I will probably explode. I get that all the time. Be a good example of this or a good example of that! Who wants to be an example of something all the time?"

Emily and Rebecca didn't say anything. Julie was more angry than they had first thought.

"I wish her mother wouldn't drag her along to the nursing home, trying to make her fit in," Emily said. "She's always so negative and whiny. She acts like her cat just died."

"Her cat actually did run away," Rebecca said. "That's what her brother told me. The day before she accused us of stealing her CD player, her cat ran away."

"I'd feel bad if any of my cats ran away," Julie said with concern.

"Don't feel too sorry," Rebecca replied. "Her brother said Clarice never fed the cat, never petted it or did anything nice. He said he didn't blame the cat for taking off."

"I'd run away too if Clarice was my owner," Emily said. "First time that door opened, I'd be gone and not look back."

Emily and Rebecca laughed. Julie smiled, but then looked serious.

"I suppose we shouldn't be talking this way about Clarice," Julie said, feeling a stab of guilt. "I feel sorry for her cat."

"That's because you're animal-crazy," Emily replied. Everyone knew Julie had a huge soft heart for animals. She had three cats, two dogs, two turtles and a duck. She would have had lots more animals if her parents would have given their permission.

The doorbell rang. The girls looked at each other and shrugged their shoulders.

"We need to be friendly to her," Julie said without enthusiasm. Secretly she felt bad because she knew she was supposed to be loving and responsible like the Bible said, but inside she didn't feel very loving. Her father was the pastor of Springdale Community Church, and Julie had been a Christian ever since she could remember. She had always assumed that she would be consistently kind and caring and a good friend.

But lately, it hadn't been so easy to be nice all the time. For some reason she just didn't feel as nice as she used to feel, and she worried about it. She knew what the Bible said about loving others. She also knew that whether people said it or not, they expected her, as a pastor's daughter, to be a shining example of a young girl, as her mother said. She was almost twelve years old. She wanted to be a good example, but when she was with Clarice, all her resolve just seemed to float out the window.

"I'm going to be nice to Clarice whether I feel like it or not," Julie announced firmly.

Julie led the others out of her room. Downstairs, Mrs. Brown and Mrs. Smoot were busy talking. Julie looked cautiously around the room.

"Where's Clarice?" Julie asked.

"She's being a real slowpoke today," Mrs. Smoot announced loudly with a hint of disgust in her voice. She was a tall, large woman who wore bright, flowery dresses. She jangled with big dangling earrings, shiny bracelets and several gold necklaces.

"Just let me get the keys to the van," Mrs. Brown said. "All the quilting and craft supplies are already packed."

"Julie, may I have a word with you?" Mrs. Smoot asked. Julie walked over. The big woman looked into Julie's face and began whispering. "I do hope you'll be friends with Clarice today. She had a bad time at the church youth group last week and said some of the other girls weren't very nice to her and said some untrue things about her."

"Oh, really?" Julie replied.

"I know that as a pastor's daughter you've been brought up differently than that," the large woman said. "Clarice is shy and a very sensitive girl. I was hoping that you could reach out to her, sort of as an example for the other girls. I know your mother thought you were good at helping the newcomers feel included."

"I know my mother thinks that." Julie tried to smile. Inside she began to fume again. She almost opened her mouth to say something, but clenched her teeth instead.

"I knew you would help out," Mrs. Smoot beamed. Mrs. Brown opened the front door.

Julie and the other girls walked outside. It was late spring and a beautiful day outside. The sky was dotted with a few clouds. Everything was spring green. Julie suddenly wished she could just go riding on her bike and have a picnic or do something fun outdoors.

"Don't dawdle, Julie!" her mother called. Julie shook her head and moved dutifully forward.

Clarice was leaning against the long white van, biting her nails. She rolled her eyes when she saw Julie and the other two girls. The tall girl had stringy red hair that often looked oily and flat, as if she didn't wash it enough. She was quite skinny. Her arms looked bony and thin. The first time she had seen her, Julie thought Clarice was getting over the flu or something because she was so pale. Later she found out that she always looked like that. Her face was also rather plain, even though she had several freckles.

"Hi, Clarice." Julie tried to sound pleasant.

"Whatever," Clarice responded as if she were the most bored person on the whole entire earth.

"I want Mrs. Smoot to sit up front with me," Mrs. Brown said as she hurried up to the van.

"Sure." Julie looked at Clarice and waited. Mrs. Smoot got in the front passenger door.

"We've got to get in the back, Clarice," Rebecca blurted out. "Quit leaning on the door."

"I'm moving," Clarice shot back at Rebecca. "It's not like this is an ambulance. Those old people will keep. They've already lived a zillion years, anyway."

She slowly stepped away from the sliding door of the van. Julie turned the handle and pushed as the door slid open. Rebecca and Emily quickly got inside and took the first bench seat. Clarice climbed in and looked at the two girls in the first seat. Rebecca had put her right knee across the seat so it looked full even though another person could have easily sat there.

"I don't want to sit with you all anyway," Clarice muttered to Rebecca.

Clarice sat down in the second seat with a sigh. She immediately stuck her legs out on the seat. Julie looked at the outstretched legs and understood.

"You can sit here with us," Rebecca offered as she noticed Clarice's legs.

"I'll sit back here." Julie slid into the third seat. She wanted to sit with her friends, but she knew her mother would say something later if they all sat together and Clarice sat by herself. Julie looked up. As she expected, her mother was watching the situation from the rear-view mirror.

Mrs. Brown backed out of the driveway. Julie sat alone in the third seat and looked at her friends ahead of her. She buckled her seat belt.

"I didn't tell you to sit there." Clarice smiled crookedly.

"I know that," Julie said. "I'm fine. I think I'll stretch my legs out myself. It's more comfortable."

"Suit yourself," Clarice spat out.

"Did you bring your CD player today?" Rebecca asked.

"No, I didn't," Clarice replied, her eyes flashing.

"We heard it turned up in your father's trunk," Emily added.

"Yeah . . ." Clarice mumbled. No one said anything for a moment. Julie saw her mom looking at them in the rear-view mirror. Julie sighed, knowing what her mom was thinking.

"I'm sorry your cat ran away," Julie said as she turned sideways in the seat.

"She was a crummy cat anyway," Clarice said bitterly. "She wasn't a friendly cat. She was friendly when she was a kitty, but when she got older, she was mean. I don't care. I didn't even know she was gone. I'm still not sure what day she ran away. Tommy was the one who noticed she was gone."

Rebecca and Emily looked at each other. Rebecca covered her mouth, trying to hide her reaction.

"Well, I know I would feel bad if one of my cats disappeared," Julie said.

"I'd like to disappear," Clarice said. "My mother knows I hate going to that stupid old folks' home. I don't see why she made me come. She said I couldn't have television for a week if I didn't put my time in. It really is unfair."

"The people at the Manor House don't like it if you call it an old folks' home," Rebecca said.

"Well, that's what it is," Clarice snapped back. "It's full of old people. Old *sick* people. My mom said an old man there died last night."

"I heard that too," Emily said. "Mr. Binton had a heart attack."

"They all look like they could drop dead any second."

Clarice shook her head. "I'm just glad my grandparents live in another state. They're old, but we only have to see them on holidays."

"You don't like to see your grandparents?" Emily asked in surprise.

"I like my grandfather Smoot okay," Clarice said. "He's nice to me. But the other ones are grouchy most of the time. And when you go to their house, they only have one television and you have to watch all the stupid TV shows that they want to watch, nothing that I want to watch. Where're your brothers? Did they get time off for good behavior or did they just sneak away?"

"They're in Colorado at a ranch," Julie tried to keep her voice even. "It's a guys' trip. Our dads and our brothers all went together."

"Yeah," Rebecca added enviously. "They're getting to ride horses and pan for gold and have lots of fun."

"I wish I was in Colorado." Clarice looked longingly out the window at the passing scenery.

"I wish I was there too," Julie agreed. "I love horses. My mom was really glad my dad got to go because he works so hard."

"My dad works hard too," Clarice said flatly. "He's hardly ever home. My mom says he's a workaholic. He just says he's busy."

"That's too bad," Julie commented.

"What's too bad?" Clarice demanded.

"That your father is so busy," Julie said slowly.

Clarice frowned at her. "He's doing okay. He has a really important job. He makes a lot of money. He says he wants to buy a boat so we can go to the lake, ride the boat and go fishing."

"Boats can be fun," Emily said, trying to be nice.

"I like fishing," Rebecca added pleasantly.

"I don't like boats and I hate fishing," Clarice grumbled. "My uncle and aunt took me fishing once and it was awful. The fish were stinky and slimy. The bait smelled bad. I hate stinky things. That's why I don't like going to the old folks' home. It smells bad in there."

"Sometimes it sort of smells like a hospital," Julie agreed.

"It's not just the medicine smells. It's the old people themselves," Clarice said quickly. "They smell bad."

"They do not!" Emily said indignantly.

"Well, some of them smell bad," Clarice insisted. "If you don't notice that, your nose must not work. Last time we were there, that one old woman in the wheelchair had a diaper on and it was leaking! Can you imagine being old and having to wear diapers, and then have them start stinking, just like you were a little baby? Yuck! Don't tell me that didn't smell bad. I was there."

"We know you were there," Rebecca retorted. "We heard you complain about it all the way home."

"That was Mrs. Snyder." Julie nodded her head as she remembered.

"She has a problem."

"You're not kidding she has a problem," Clarice exclaimed. "They all have problems. There was that one really old woman who sat in the corner and talked to herself the whole time while she was knitting. She's crazy as a hoot owl."

"You mean the lady they call Aunt Esther?" Julie asked.

"Yeah, that little short one about a hundred and twenty years old," Clarice replied. "She looked like a leathery prune, she's so old. And she's real short. Did you see her stand up? My little brother is bigger than her, and he's only nine."

"She's a hundred and two," Rebecca said. "How do you expect her to look at that age? She's the same size as me, only I'm not bent over like her."

"Her eyes still twinkle," Julie said. "And even though she's really old, she has a cheerful smile and cheerful wrinkles."

"Cheerful wrinkles?" Clarice grunted again. "Maybe she tells herself jokes when she's talking to herself. I hate being around those old crazy people."

"If you hate it so much, then why did you come?" Rebecca asked in exasperation.

"Because my mother *made* me," Clarice whispered back. "She threatened to take away my TV and phone. It was pure blackmail. Close to child abuse, if you ask me."

"You have your own TV in your room?" Emily asked in surprise.

"A thirty-two-inch TV," Clarice said proudly. "And I aim to hang onto it. That's the only reason I'm here, believe me."

"I believe you," Julie said flatly.

"Me too." Rebecca nodded, putting a hand across her mouth, trying to hide her smile.

Clarice stared suspiciously at Rebecca and Emily. Then she turned to Julie.

"I bet you only come because your mother makes you," she said to Julie.

"That's not true," Emily said defensively.

"Yeah, who are you to judge Julie's motives?" Rebecca demanded.

"I'm not talking to you guys," Clarice shot back. She turned to Julie. "Tell me the truth. You're only coming because your mother made you, right?"

Julie was taken by surprise by the suddenness of Clarice's accusation. She wasn't sure how to answer. She opened her mouth but no words came out.

"See, I told you she didn't want to come," Clarice announced proudly to the others.

"You didn't even give her a chance to speak," Rebecca protested. "Julie is coming because she wants to help out. Besides, we're on a case today."

"A case?" Clarice asked. "What are you talking about?"

"A mystery case," Emily said. "One of the ladies at the Manor House, Mrs. Babbage, wants us to work for her as detectives."

"Detectives?" Clarice asked. "Detectives for what?"

"We're not sure if we can help her yet," Julie added quickly. "But she read in the newspapers about some other cases we helped solve, and she's asked for our help."

"Yeah, some people call us the Home School Detectives," Rebecca said.

"Yeah, I've heard all about it." Clarice tried to act like she wasn't impressed. "You solved some old robbery and helped some computer nerd one time, and stuff like that. You guys are a *very* big deal. Nancy Drew is really jealous, I'm sure. So why does this old lady want your help?"

"Mrs. Babbage wants our help." Julie paused. "But she didn't say why yet."

"And besides, it's confidential," Emily said. "All our detective consultations are private."

"Well, it looks like she's ready to talk now." Clarice pointed to a woman standing on the sidewalk in front of the Manor House.

"That's Mrs. Babbage," Julie said in surprise. An old woman in a simple blue dress and thick black shoes watched the van closely while waving her hand. Her face was lined with worry.

"We'd better see what she wants." Julie got up and slid open the sliding door. Mrs. Babbage was already walking down the sidewalk. Clarice and the other girls got out.

"Here she comes," Clarice whispered. "I just hope she doesn't smell funny."

"Clarice!" Julie hissed.

"Mind your own business," Clarice whispered back.

"Julie, I've been waiting for you!" Mrs. Babbage said breathlessly. "We must talk right away!"

"I need to help my mom take the supplies in," Julie said.

"Of course, of course," Mrs. Babbage nodded. "But we can talk right after that, can't we? You will help me, won't you?"

"Julie, can you help me?" her mother called from the rear of the van.

"Coming!" Julie smiled at Mrs. Babbage. The four girls walked to the rear of the van. The old woman followed. For a moment, her worried face relaxed.

"Can I help carry something?" the woman asked.

"Don't you touch a thing, Mrs. Babbage," Mrs. Brown said. "These girls are very strong and more than able to help out. Julie is my extra special helper this week because my husband and oldest son are gone on a vacation."

"To the ranch in Colorado," Mrs. Babbage said. "I've heard all about it. But I would like to impose on your daughter and her companions myself, if that's all right with you, once you get the craft room set up. I need some help on a matter."

"I'm sure they'll be glad to help." Mrs. Brown handed a box full of cloth patches to Clarice. "Let's get these supplies inside first."

"I insist on paying them for their services." Mrs. Babbage followed Mrs. Brown, Julie and the others into the Springdale Manor House.

"Well, that solves one mystery," Clarice said to Julie and the other girls as she walked inside the Manor House hall carrying her box.

"What do you mean?" Julie asked.

"Now I know why you're here," Clarice said smugly. "You're in it for the money. I know about Mrs. Babbage. She's really rich. My mother said that Mrs. Babbage is one of the richest people in town."

"Well, even if she is well off, I am not doing this for the money," Julie replied hotly. Her cheeks burned. She was about to say more, but they had entered the big recreation room where several senior citizens had already gathered, waiting for the arrival of the quilting, needlework and other craft supplies. Several other people from the Springdale Community Church were already there, helping get ready. Julie plopped her box down on a table. Mrs. Babbage walked over.

"Can we talk in private now?" the woman asked.

"I know I'm ready to hear about this case," Clarice said

eagerly.

"Let's go then," the older woman said to the four girls.

"But Clarice—" Rebecca blurted out.

"Let's go, Rebecca," Clarice scolded. "We've already made Mrs. Babbage wait long enough."

"I hope you can help me with my problem," Mrs. Babbage said approvingly to Clarice. She then reached down and took Clarice by the arm. "Please follow me, girls." The old woman began walking, pulling Clarice along with her.

"She can't come!" Rebecca whispered in protest.

Julie shook her head helplessly as she watched the old woman talk to Clarice as they walked down the hall. The three girls ran to catch up.

Chapter Two

Herbert's Gold Watch

"What are we going to do?" Rebecca demanded to Julie as they hurried down the hall.

"Yeah, what?" Emily added. Both girls often looked to Julie for leadership since she was the oldest. "Can you believe how she's sticking her nose in our business like that?"

"I don't know what to do." Julie felt anger churn inside. She was already mad several times over for Clarice's remarks and accusations. But she had been totally stunned when Mrs. Babbage assumed Clarice was part of the Home School Detectives.

Clarice looked over her shoulder and smiled very sweetly at the other three girls following behind. Then she turned back around.

"She thinks this is funny," Julie whispered angrily. "She knows what she is doing."

Mrs. Babbage stopped at a door. She fumbled with her keys.

"Let me help you, Mrs. Babbage," Clarice offered very sweetly.

"You are so polite," Mrs. Babbage said. Clarice just smiled again. The door swung open. Mrs. Babbage led them inside. When all four girls were inside, she closed the door.

The room was like a small apartment. A couch and overstuffed chair filled the first living area. Behind a counter was a compact kitchen. A door opened beyond the cozy living room to a bedroom. Clarice sniffed the air cautiously.

"Don't you need to join the others back in the recreation room?" Julie asked Clarice loudly. She stared angrily at the redheaded girl. "I know you don't want your mother to worry about you."

"Yeah, you don't want your mother to worry, Clarice," Rebecca added.

"She saw us leave with Mrs. Babbage," Clarice said.

"But this is a *private* matter," Emily added flatly.

"And Mrs. Babbage wants to talk to us right away, before we help with the crafts," Clarice added with a serious voice. "Don't you, Mrs. Babbage?"

"Yes, the sooner the better." Mrs. Babbage had a determined sparkle in her eyes. "Would you care for any sodas or juice?" Mrs. Babbage walked quickly over to the small refrigerator in the corner of the kitchen.

"No, thank you, Mrs. Babbage," Julie said, still feeling flustered. She looked at the other girls with a warning glance. She shook her head to warn them not to accept a soda. Her mind was racing, thinking of how to shut out

Clarice or get rid of her.

"I'd like a soda," Clarice said loudly. "What do you have?"

Mrs. Babbage looked inside the refrigerator.

"I have grape and orange," she said. "I thought I had some colas, but my grandchildren must have finished those off on their last visit."

"I'll have a grape," Clarice said. "Grape always hits the spot when we're on a case."

"What about the rest of you?"

Rebecca hesitated. "I'd like a grape too, I guess." She looked at Julie, who shook her head again. Emily looked at Julie, then at the sodas longingly.

"I'll have an orange," Emily said. Julie frowned at her friend. Emily looked defensive. "Well, I'm thirsty and Rebecca was having one."

"Sure you don't want a soda, Julie?" Mrs. Babbage asked. "I've got more than enough."

"No, thank you." Julie glared at her friends as they began sipping their sodas. She felt betrayed. She knew they had understood her intention.

"Now let's hear all about your problem." Clarice sat down. "We really want to help. We talked about you on the way over here, but I didn't quite understand exactly what you wanted us to do."

"Well, how could you, child?" the old woman asked. "I haven't had a chance to tell you yet."

"And that is the reason," Clarice said dramatically to Julie, "that you shouldn't jump to conclusions."

"I didn't jump to any conclusions," Julie sputtered indignantly. "Mrs. Babbage, Clarice doesn't know anything about this or—"

"Then let me tell you all because I've been worried sick, just sick," the old woman said quickly. She stood up and clenched her hands together. Her eyes teared up. "It's my husband's watch."

"What about it?" Clarice asked

"It's missing, and I absolutely must find it, before . . ." The woman stopped talking as she anxiously looked off into the air.

"Before what?" Clarice asked.

"Well . . ." the old woman said uncomfortably. "Before . . . it is permanently lost . . . I just want it back. It's very valuable to me. You will help me find Herbert's watch, won't you? As I said, I will pay you for your efforts. I know how hard it is for a young person to earn money."

"We will try to help you, Mrs. Babbage," Julie said quickly, glaring at Clarice. "And we don't expect any money."

"No, I insist on paying you," Mrs. Babbage said.

"We wouldn't think of it, Mrs. Babbage," Emily said. "We're glad to help, and we don't want any money."

Clarice looked from girl to girl with surprise and suspicion.

"If Mrs. Babbage *insists* on paying us I think we should respect her wishes," Clarice said to Emily. "After all, I'm sure this is a valuable watch. Exactly how much were you thinking of paying? I get twenty dollars for baby-sitting on Friday nights at the Greenbaums."

"Well, I want to be fair . . ."

"Absolutely not!" Julie almost shouted.

"What?" Mrs. Babbage asked Julie. The old woman

looked confused and surprised at Julie's outburst.

"I'm sorry." Julie felt embarrassed. "What I meant is that we don't want any money at all. We will help you for free, won't we?" Julie looked at Rebecca and Emily. The two girls nodded their agreement quickly.

"We don't charge money for something like this, Mrs. Babbage," Emily said.

"We sure don't," Rebecca added, frowning at Clarice.

"I was only trying to respect Mrs. Babbage's wishes." Clarice looked at the other girls as if she was being unfairly accused.

"So you want us to find a watch?" Julie asked Mrs. Babbage.

"It's a gold pocket watch that belonged to my husband, Herbert," Mrs. Babbage said. She rushed to the kitchenette and opened a drawer. She returned holding a small gold watch chain. "This chain used to be attached to the watch. Herbert's father gave him the watch on our wedding day. Herbert carried it all his life, even when it stopped working. He had it fixed several times. The main spring was bad."

"You mean you want us to find a watch that doesn't even work?" Clarice asked in surprise. "Why don't you just buy a new watch?"

"The watch is important to me because it belonged to my late husband." Mrs. Babbage looked at the limp watch chain with forlorn eyes. "I never even liked it all that much. We used to argue over it, in fact, when he was still living . . . I mean . . . oh, dear . . ."

"You argued over it?" Clarice repeated. "Why?"

"That's not the important thing," Mrs. Babbage said. "What I meant to say was that the watch had great sentimental value for Herbert and for me. I must have it back. It must not fall into the wrong hands."

"Wrong hands?" Clarice asked with interest. "Is there some secret in the watch? Is it some kind of spy watch? Your husband wasn't a spy, was he?"

"A spy?" Mrs. Babbage asked in surprise. "He was an accountant."

"But you said the watch shouldn't fall into the wrong hands. What did you mean?" Clarice demanded. The old woman looked confused for a moment. She looked at the floor and took a deep breath.

"That was a poor choice of words," Mrs. Babbage said slowly. She turned away from Clarice's curious eyes and looked at Julie. "Can you help me find it?"

"Do you want us to look around here?" Julie asked.

"No, no," the old woman said. "It's not in here. That's the problem. I had it in the Community Room last night. I was going to have Mr. Binton put the chain back on the watch. He was a jeweler, you know. We had finished eating dinner. He told me he could fix it."

"Mr. Binton?" Clarice asked. "Isn't he the dead guy?"

"Well . . . yes, he . . . passed away last night of a heart attack," Mrs. Babbage said sadly. "This is what happened. I came back to my room to get the watch and chain after supper. But when I returned to the Community Room, Mr. Binton's two sons were talking to him."

"What were they talking about?" Clarice demanded.

"Good heavens, how should I know?" Mrs. Babbage said. "I didn't eavesdrop, though one of his sons seemed upset. They've run the jewelry store since Mr. Binton retired. I sat down on the blue couch, waiting while they talked."

"But you didn't hear what they said?" Clarice asked with disappointment.

"Let her finish the story," Julie said to Clarice. "We'll never get anywhere if you keep interrupting."

"I'm only trying to help," Clarice whined.

"I'm sorry, Mrs. Babbage," Julie said to the woman. "You were waiting for Mr. Binton to fix your watch and then what happened?"

"Mr. Binton and his sons began to argue, though I don't know why," Mrs. Babbage said. "Mr. Binton was an emotional man. He did get upset rather easily. Some men are like that. Anyway, instead of helping me, he went back to his room with his sons without saying a word to me. Well, I waited and waited. I really wanted my watch fixed. So I finally got up and went to his room."

"And you found him dead!" Clarice jumped in.

"No, he died later," Mrs. Babbage said. "But when I got to his door, I heard more arguing. I was going to knock, but then decided to wait because I could hear loud voices. At that moment, the door burst open and his son Roger was standing there. He stared at me, then left without a word, followed by the other son, John. I looked in and saw Mr. Binton sitting by his bed, his face wet with tears."

"He was crying?" Clarice asked.

"That's what tears mean, Clarice," Rebecca said condescendingly.

"Well, you don't usually see old guys cry," Clarice said. "I've never seen my dad cry. I've seen him get really mad lots of times."

"I can't imagine why," Julie muttered.

"What did you say?" Clarice asked Julie.

"Nothing. Let Mrs. Babbage finish."

"Well, I felt uncomfortable seeing Mr. Binton cry," Mrs. Babbage said. "He looked up and saw me, unfortunately. I walked away without saying a word. I knew that he and his sons had had problems before, and it was a source of grief to him. They disagree over business and other family matters."

"But you just left him there, crying like that?" Clarice asked.

"Well, as I said, I didn't want to interfere," Mrs. Babbage replied. "I felt awkward seeing him so upset. So I went back to the Community Room, holding my watch. It was a night for arguments. Ms. Dearborn and Mr. Schoons were arguing in the hallway, right out in public. She is the manager of the Manor House and he works for the hospital. The Manor House staff and the hospital staff have had several public disagreements lately, and it's very unprofessional in my opinion."

"Disagreements about what?" Clarice asked eagerly.

"Over the level of care at the Manor House and who is responsible for mistakes that have occurred," the woman said. "The hospital nurses and the Manor House nurses do not get along. The Manor House has been in trouble with state inspectors recently and has even been fined over health-care violations. There have been serious disagreements over what treatments residents received or did not receive. Ms. Dearborn fired the head nurse and two other nurses here a few weeks ago after the Manor House was cited for some serious violations. Some residents say Ms. Dearborn may even lose her job. I think it's been very unprofessional, and the residents here think these public disagreements are atrocious. I have complained personally to the state inspectors as well as to Ms. Dearborn."

"But what about your lost watch?" Julie asked.

"Well, I had given up on Mr. Binton since he was so upset," Mrs. Babbage said. "I did not speak to Mr. Schoons or Ms. Dearborn as I passed them in the hallway. They tried to act as if they weren't arguing, but I had already heard them."

"They were acting suspicious then?" Clarice asked.

"Let her finish, Clarice!" Julie said impatiently. "What happened next?" she asked Mrs. Babbage.

"Well, I wasn't sure what to do," the old woman said. "I sat down on the couch in the Community Room. I was going to go back to my room when I saw Mr. Binton coming down the hallway. I smiled at him, and he smiled at me. His eyes were still red from crying. He looked very discouraged and sad. Anyway, he sat down, and I gave him the watch and the loose chain. He didn't say a word, and I didn't want to embarrass him. He had a little pair of pliers. He was a very gentle and kind man. He treated my watch with great care. He had just started to work on the chain when he fell over onto the floor."

"You mean he died right in front of you?" Clarice asked with surprise.

"He didn't die at that moment," Mrs. Babbage said. "I called out for help, of course. Then I leaned down to see if I could help him. He tried to whisper something in my ear. I was listening when the nurses rushed up and took over. I was quite upset, of course. He was having his heart attack at that moment. The whole situation was awful. The ambulance came from the hospital across the street, and they worked on him right away, but he died a few hours later at the hospital.

"Wow!" Clarice said softly.

"So what happened to your watch?" Julie asked.

"It got lost once Mr. Binton fell over," the old woman said. "But you see, I didn't realize it was gone until later. I was so upset at the moment, I just forgot about my watch."

"That's so sad." Julie nodded her head sympathetically.

"I was in the Community Room talking with Mrs. Gillworst and some of my other friends about poor Mr. Binton for over an hour," the old woman said. "When I got back to my room, I realized I had forgotten all about my watch. I hurried back to the Community Room and looked on the floor around the couch. I found the chain on the floor, but not the watch. It must be found."

"Someone probably picked it up, don't you think?" Julie asked.

"That's precisely what I'm afraid of," Mrs. Babbage said heavily.

"Why?" Rebecca asked. "Do you think they won't return it? Maybe they don't know it's yours."

"They will know it is mine because my husband's name is on the inside cover." The old woman sounded weary. "Our names and the date of our wedding, as well as the names of our four children, are all engraved inside the case lid. I begged him not to do that, but he insisted. He was very proud of our children: Sarah, Susan, Sally and Sharon. Their birthdays are listed right next to their names. He insisted on putting in their birthdays even though I asked him not to do that. Herbert could be a stubborn man, even if my feelings suffered." The old woman sighed sadly.

"If your name is in the watch, whoever finds it will probably return it," Julie offered. "They'll see the names inside the lid and know it belongs to you."

"Yeah, who would want some old watch that doesn't even work?" Clarice asked.

"Listen, I must have my watch back, before they find it . . ." The old woman looked at the floor. She covered her face with her hands and sobbed. The four girls watched her uncomfortably. She sobbed for what seemed like several minutes. Julie found a box of tissues and waited. When the old woman looked up, Julie handed her a tissue.

Mrs. Babbage caught her breath. "I'm sorry. This has been very upsetting for me. I did not sleep at all last night. I simply must have my watch back. Please help me find it. Let me show you where I saw it last."

The old woman quickly turned toward the door and walked out. She waited for the girls to follow and then shut the door behind them. She walked more quickly down the hall than Julie and the other girls expected.

"She's really upset about that watch," Julie whispered to Rebecca.

"No kidding," Rebecca replied.

"She's not telling us something," Clarice said flatly. "No one gets that worried about some old watch that doesn't even work. Something seems fishy to me about this whole thing."

"No one asked you what you thought," Emily said. "In fact, you shouldn't even be here. You aren't part of our detective team. Is she, Julie?"

"Well, I don't remember inviting you," Julie said grimly.

She looked sideways at Clarice. "Mrs. Babbage sure walks fast for someone her age. It does seem like she is keeping a secret. Or maybe she is worried about something else."

The old woman walked down the hallway across the big open Community Room to a blue couch. She turned and waited for the girls to reach her.

"This is where we were sitting," the old woman said. "The watch is about two inches in diameter. It has a worn gold cover."

Julie bent down and looked under the couch. The other three girls knelt down beside her.

"I don't see it under the couch," Julie said.

"Maybe someone kicked it," Rebecca said. "It would slide on this hard tile floor just like a hockey puck."

"I thought someone might have kicked it," Mrs. Babbage agreed. She stood stiffly, her old gray eyes searching the floor.

"Maybe you should sit down," Julie said to the older woman. "You must be tired."

"I'll go back to my room," Mrs. Babbage said wearily. "I need to take my medicine. But please bring me the watch the instant you find it. Will you promise?"

"Yes, of course," Julie said. "We'll bring it right to you."

"Good." The old woman looked at the floor once more, biting a knuckle on her right hand. She shook her head, turned and then walked away.

"Let's spread out from this point in four directions," Julie said. "I'll check under the couch cushions first."

"What about Clarice?" Rebecca asked.

"We can use all the help we can get," Julie said. "But if you find it, Clarice, bring it right over to us."

"Maybe I will." Clarice stuck out her tongue at Rebecca. Before Rebecca could say a word, Clarice turned away, acting as if she was searching the floor.

The four girls searched for thirty minutes in the big Community Room, looking under every couch and chair and table, oblivious to the activity going on around them. They gathered back at the couch to talk.

"I found two dollars and three cents in the couch," Julie said. "And two cough drops, but no watch."

"This is boring." Clarice tugged absent-mindedly on a long strand of her stringy hair. "Besides, my knees are getting sore from being on this hard floor."

"We don't need your help anyway," Rebecca said.

"Well, I have another idea." Immediately Clarice walked off.

"Where's she going?" Rebecca asked sullenly.

"Who cares?" Emily asked. "I'm glad she's gone."

"She's going down the hall toward Mrs. Babbage's room." Julie looked alarmed.

"Do you think she's going back to bother Mrs. Babbage?"

"We can't let her do that!" Rebecca blurted out.

The three girls jumped up and ran after Clarice. When they reached the hallway, Clarice was already approaching Mrs. Babbage's door.

"Let her rest, Clarice!" Julie called out. The three girls ran up to her.

"I have an important question." Clarice was just about to knock on the door when they heard a crashing sound inside the room. The girls froze. Julie then knocked on the door.

"Mrs. Babbage, are you all right?" Julie yelled. "Mrs. Babbage?"

Clarice turned the doorknob and pushed it open. She ran inside.

"Mrs. Babbage!" Clarice said loudly. Then she looked in the bedroom and screamed. The other girls rushed up beside her. Clarice's shaking arm pointed ahead of them. A broken lamp was lying near the bed. On the floor, they saw a pair of legs and feet with heavy dark shoes sticking out from behind the bed.

"Mrs. Babbage!" Julie cried out. Clarice screamed again and again.

Chapter Three

Aunt Esther's Gentle Help

"She's dead! She's dead!" Clarice moaned, leaning against the hallway wall after they left the room.

"She's not dead." Julie's voice cracked. "But something's very wrong." Julie had called 911 immediately while Rebecca ran to get help from the nursing-home staff. The children had waited by the old woman's side until the adults arrived a few minutes later. The small room had become crowded, so they had stepped out into the hall.

"Are you sure she's not dead?" Clarice asked Julie, as if looking for reassurance. "How do you know? Are you sure?"

"Because I felt her pulse when she was on the floor," Julie said.

"You touched her?" Clarice asked in surprise. She looked up through bleary eyes. Some strands of her red hair stuck to her pale, wet cheek. Clarice looked paler than ever.

"Yes," Julie said. "She had a pulse, and she was breathing. So she wasn't dead. I heard someone ask Nurse Pierce, from the hospital emergency room, and she said Mrs. Babbage's pulse rate was erratic."

Clarice's fears and tears irritated Julie. She wasn't sure Clarice was being genuine at first. But after a while it was obvious that Clarice was truly upset. Julie didn't know if Clarice's tough talk was a kind of act or if she was a big baby. Not knowing what to make of Clarice's reaction added to Julie's anger.

The door to Mrs. Babbage's room swung open. A man and a woman in white uniforms pushed a rolling stretcher out of the room. Mrs. Babbage's nose and mouth were covered with a clear oxygen mask. A small plastic bag of clear liquid was hanging on a metal pole next to the stretcher. Plastic tubes ran from the hanging bag down to the stretcher. One was attached to Mrs. Babbage's arm.

"Is she going to be all right, Nurse Pierce?" Julie asked a stocky woman in a nurse's uniform.

"We're doing our best," the nurse replied seriously. "We've got to get her to the emergency room."

Several Manor House residents had gathered in the hallway and talked quietly. A man in a wheelchair watched intently as the stretcher passed him. People in the hall moved silently out of the way, whispering to each other. A tall woman in a dark blue business coat walked out of the room quickly behind the rolling stretcher. She looked very unhappy. She stared at the man in the wheelchair and frowned. The man smiled halfheartedly back at the woman.

"That's Ms. Dearborn, the manager," Julie whispered to Rebecca.

"Please be careful, Nurse Pierce," Ms. Dearborn called out. "I will notify Mrs. Babbage's family."

"Will you be doing that today, Ms. Dearborn?" the nurse asked, an edge to her voice.

A flare of anger filled the tall woman's face. She started to speak but caught herself when she noticed the children and the others in the hallway watching her. She took a deep breath, nodded her head, and walked back into Mrs. Babbage's room.

The man in the wheelchair rolled himself down the hall until he was about ten feet away from the children. He had watched the exchange between the nurse and Ms. Dearborn with intense interest. He rolled his wheelchair so the back was flat against the wall next to a large white pot with a green bushy plant.

Clarice put her hand up to her mouth as she watched them wheel Mrs. Babbage away. Julie looked at Clarice and scowled.

"She's taking this pretty hard," Rebecca said softly to Julie and Emily.

"Yeah, she's really upset," Emily agreed. "I guess everyone around here is upset."

"Well, it serves Clarice right," Julie blurted out. "I mean, no one asked her to come along with us. She just butted in, even when she knew we didn't want her to come. She just had to stick her nose in our business. And now she's sorry she did."

"Ssssshhhh! She'll hear you!" Emily whispered to Julie.

"I don't care if she does hear me," Julie said defiantly, in an even louder voice.

"I thought we were going to be nice to Clarice," Rebecca

offered, surprised by Julie's tone.

"Well, I'm all out of *nice*." Julie looked angry. "All she does is whine and complain and interfere in our business. Then something bad happens, and she falls apart. Well, I've had it. There's a limit to how nice you can be to some people. I don't care what my mother says."

"It's not just your mother," Emily said. "Even God says we're supposed—"

"Don't tell me what God says," Julie snapped, her eyes flashing. "You think I don't know what God says? I'm a pastor's kid. I've heard it all my life, and I *know* what God says. I've probably memorized more Bible verses than both of you two put together."

"Well, like your father always says, knowing and obeying are two different . . ." Rebecca stopped talking when she saw the fire glaring out of Julie's eyes. The hallway got very quiet, except for Clarice's sobbing by the doorway.

Rebecca and Emily stared at Julie with concern. Julie was usually soft-spoken and rarely critical. But now their friend's face was hardened and tense as she stared at the sobbing girl.

"Will you quit acting like a big baby?" Julie burst out. Clarice looked up through teary eyes. When she saw the angry look on Julie's face, she began to cry even louder. Emily and Rebecca looked at Julie with even more surprise.

"Are you okay, Julie?" Emily whispered uneasily.

"No, I am not okay." Julie felt a hard lump in her throat and anger churn in her stomach. "Did you see Mrs. Babbage lying there? What if she dies? What if we did something to upset her or something?"

"She was already upset," Rebecca said. "We were trying to help her."

"She seemed calmer when she went back to her room," Rebecca said.

"I don't think we helped her much," Julie replied. "And Clarice just butts into our business and then cries when things don't go her way."

"Maybe she's more sensitive than we thought," Rebecca said. "All her tough talk could be an act. I have a cousin who talks like she doesn't care about stuff, but my mom says she talks that way because she really feels insecure and lonely."

"Yeah, she actually could be trying to cover her feelings," Emily said.

"If she's really so sensitive, she could win an Academy Award for her performances," Julie said in disgust. She couldn't believe her friends were being taken in. "Her crying could be a big act, too. Who knows with her?"

"You know, if Clarice hadn't come back to the room, we might not have even heard Mrs. Babbage fall," Emily said. "Finding her so soon may have helped save her life."

"Sure, take her side in it," Julie accused. "Poor, sensitive, misunderstood Clarice is a big hero now for butting into our business."

"No one said that." Emily shrugged her shoulders.

"Yeah, Julie," Rebecca added. "I know you're upset, but you don't have to bite Emily's head off."

"I'm not . . ." Julie looked down, her eyes filled with tears. She bit down on her fist to try to get control. Then she took a deep breath. "I wish I hadn't come today. Clarice was right. I didn't want to come here in the first place."

The older girl's shoulders shook as she tried to hold back her emotions. Emily and Rebecca looked worried.

"You look like a girl who's been running from a tiger all night," a voice said behind Julie. Julie whirled around. She looked down. The wrinkled face of the woman they called Aunt Esther was looking up at Julie with concern and compassion. The short, old woman wore a worn pink sweater over her hunched shoulders. She was small for an adult, not any taller than Rebecca Renner. She wore wire-framed glasses. A soft quilt lay folded over her arm. The woman's ancient gray eyes were kind, yet they made Julie feel exposed, as if the woman could see all her secret thoughts.

"What did you say?" Julie asked, jerking her head suddenly backward as if she'd been hit with an invisible gust of wind.

"Sometimes those pet kitties become tigers and turn mean, don't they?" the old woman replied. "Some will chase you so hard you think they will eat you up. That's why you've got to be on the watch. When you're on the watch, the Father keeps you away from those tigers. He sends his angels to help us."

"Uh . . . I guess so." Julie stared back at the woman uncomfortably. Rebecca and Emily were still worried about their friend. Julie looked puzzled. Her mouth had dropped open.

"Are you okay, Julie?" Rebecca asked. "You look funny."

"How did you know about the cat and the tiger?" Julie asked the old woman, ignoring Rebecca's question.

"God knows all your problems, child," the old woman

said sweetly. "Just like he sent me here to help this little one. The Father showed me she's not feeling well, and he wants to love on her. The Father wants to love on all his children, did you know that? He has great big arms of love for his children. He does indeed."

"I guess . . ." Julie mumbled. The hunched-over little woman walked with short steps over to Clarice.

"This little one needs some help," the old woman said softly. "It's going to be all right, child."

The little old woman unfolded the quilt and wrapped it around Clarice's shoulders. She then hugged Clarice and patted her on the back. Julie and the other girls watched in silent suspense. Clarice's tear-filled eyes looked down into the old woman's face. Instead of pulling away, as Julie expected, Clarice sobbed louder and hugged the old woman back.

"It's going to be all right, child," the old woman said in soothing tones. "There, there . . . The Father knows."

After a few minutes, the old woman began leading the sobbing girl down the hallway. They walked side by side, the old woman cooing words of comfort and solace to the distraught girl. They sat down on a couch in the hallway near the lobby. The old woman rocked Clarice back and forth and softly patted her hair.

"What's she doing?" Julie asked in bewilderment.

"She's rocking her like a little kid," Rebecca said with surprise. "My mom used to do that to me when I was upset."

"But she's not related to Clarice." Julie still had anger in her voice.

"Well, she must be a Christian the way she talked about

God," Emily responded. "She seems real nice, like a real experienced grandmother."

"Clarice doesn't seem to mind," Rebecca added. "Look at her."

The thin girl cried on Aunt Esther's shoulder while the old woman continued to rock and pat her.

"I thought she hated old people," Julie said suspiciously.

"I think Aunt Esther likes her." Rebecca smiled.

"What was that stuff she said to you about a tiger chasing you?" Emily asked Julie. "And why did you flinch?"

"You said earlier you had dreamed about being chased, didn't you?" Rebecca asked.

"It's so weird . . ." Julie replied, shaking her head in wonder as she stared at the old woman on the couch.

"I know it's weird, but why did you jerk?" Rebecca said. "I saw that too. It looked like you saw a ghost."

"I don't see how she could know about the tiger . . . or the angel . . ." Julie said softly, as if her friends weren't even there.

"What tiger?" Emily asked. "She said a tiger chased you or something."

"A tiger did chase me," said Julie, still staring with astonishment at the old woman. "Only it wasn't a tiger at first. At first it was a cat. It was like a pet cat in my house, only it wasn't any of the cats I have now. This was a calico cat and sort of wild. At first it was friendly. But I got mad at it because I called it and it wouldn't come to me or do what I said. And so I screamed at it really loud and called it all kinds of ugly names. I never even use those words when I'm awake. But it was a stubborn cat. I called it even worse names, and then it growled at me. Then all of a sudden it started running across the room right at me, with really angry, yellow eyes. I screamed and started to run. I ran upstairs. The cat followed me, and as it started up the stairs, I turned to see if it was very close and it turned into a great big orange and black tiger."

"What are you talking about? Are you kidding us?" Rebecca asked. Julie's face was serious.

"No," Julie said. "This big, out-of-control tiger came up the stairs and chased me all around the house. I kept running away, but it got closer and closer. I climbed up the little ladder that goes up into the attic, only it was huge. It was like a great big building that was under construction. There were ladders and piles of lumber and paint buckets lying around. It didn't look anything like our attic. But the tiger kept chasing me until it cornered me at this pool of dark water. I couldn't run any farther. The tiger rushed at me, its big mouth wide open. But instead of teeth, its mouth was full of needles, like the kind they use at the doctor's office."

"Needles like in a shot?" Rebecca asked.

"I was scared to death," Julie said. "But then I saw an angel as the tiger jumped at me. I ducked down, and it leaped over me. And then I woke up."

"You mean it was a dream!" Rebecca laughed. "You had me going there. You made it sound so real. That's a really weird dream."

"It felt real when I was dreaming it," Julie replied. "I was so glad when I woke up."

"Wait a minute," Emily frowned. "It sounds like Aunt Esther knew what you dreamed."

"That's what's really weird," Julie still stared at the little old woman. "How could she know?"

"You didn't tell her about the dream?" Rebecca asked.

"I don't even know her," Julie said. "You're the first people I've told. I just had that dream this morning. Remember, I told you back in my room that I had had a bad dream."

"Wow!" Emily said. "That's awesome."

"That really is strange," Rebecca added. All three girls stared at the little old woman who continued to rock Clarice. They could hear her humming a hymn.

"A lot of unusual things have happened around here," a voice said behind them. All three girls jumped in surprise.

Julie whirled around. She looked down and saw the man in the wheelchair. She had forgotten all about him. He had rolled up right behind them without making a sound. He looked up and smiled crookedly, as if he knew secrets he wasn't telling. Without another word, he quickly turned his chair around and then rolled slowly toward Mrs. Babbage's doorway. He looked inside the room curiously. Then he looked back at the girls. He seemed to be waiting for them.

"Mrs. Babbage wouldn't want you to give up so soon." The man smiled again and then looked inside the old woman's room. "If you keep looking, who knows what else you may find out?"

Chapter Four

Mr. Carlino's Surprising Discovery

The man in the wheelchair peeped into Mrs. Babbage's room with quick, curious eyes. Julie and her friends walked over slowly. The man was relatively young compared to everyone else in the Manor House. That's what seemed odd about him. He didn't look to be older than fifty. Yet Julie felt certain that she had heard someone say that he was a resident. She had seen him several times before when she had come with the church group, only he never took part in the craft activities with the senior citizens. His curly black hair was streaked with wisps of gray. His brown eyes sparkled with life as he looked into Mrs. Babbage's room.

Julie peeked inside. Ms. Dearborn was looking on while a young woman in a short white coat swept pieces of the broken lamp into a dustpan.

"Make sure you get every piece of that, Maria," the

woman instructed. Her forehead was knotted in an unhappy frown. She held a clipboard in her hand. She turned and saw Julie. She didn't smile.

"Are you one of the children that found her?" the woman asked. Her voice almost sounded accusing. She looked down on her clipboard, reading something.

"Yes," Julie said. "My friends and I found her. Is she going to be all right?"

"I hope so," the woman said flatly. "She's quite old. They took her across the street to the hospital. I'm glad it's close. It's a real convenience when we have an emergency. You're part of the church group, aren't you?"

"Yes," Julie said. Rebecca and Emily crowded up next to Julie in the doorway. "We came to help with the craft projects and read to people, but Mrs. Babbage had asked us to help her find a missing watch."

"You were here when she fell?" the woman asked.

"We didn't see her fall," Rebecca said.

"We were outside the door," Emily added. "And we heard a crash. It must have been the lamp. Then we came inside. Clarice was the one who saw her first."

"Who are you?" Ms. Dearborn asked in a businesslike way.

"I'm Julie Brown."

"You're the pastor's daughter," Ms. Dearborn said.

"That's right," Julie said.

"And I'm Rebecca Renner."

"I'm Emily Morgan. Clarice is down the hall. She's the one who saw Mrs. Babbage first. She's still crying. But Aunt Esther is kind of hugging her."

"I should talk to her," Ms. Dearborn said.

"She was real upset." Julie looked uncertain. "But she seems to like Aunt Esther."

"Aunt Esther is everyone's grandmother," Ms. Dearborn said gently, with a friendlier tone. "She's amazing. She's one hundred and two years old and still has lots of pep, as she likes to say. If your friend is upset, being with Aunt Esther is the best place to be. Now, can you describe what happened when you entered the apartment?"

"We saw her lying on the floor," Julie pointed to the little bedroom. "It was awful. We heard the lamp crash when we were outside."

"But you didn't see her fall?" the woman asked.

"None of us saw her fall. The door was closed," Rebecca said.

Ms. Dearborn frowned. She looked down at her clipboard. She looked up the girls and was quiet. She looked down at the clipboard again. "You say you were helping her find . . . a watch?"

"She had lost a watch that had belonged to her husband," Julie said. "We said we would help her look for it. She had lost it last night, out in the Community Room. Mr. Binton was trying to put the chain back on the watch when he had his heart attack."

"A very unfortunate incident." Ms. Dearborn stood stiffly. "Many of the residents were upset. Mrs. Babbage was extremely agitated. Of course, she was there when he had his heart attack."

"In all the commotion, she lost track of the watch," Julie said. "She showed us where they had been sitting when she had last seen the watch."

"But we didn't find it," Rebecca said.

"Mrs. Babbage said she felt tired and went back to her room while we were looking for the watch," Emily added.

"So you came down here to tell her that you didn't find the watch, and that's when you heard the crash?" Ms. Dearborn asked.

"That's pretty much what happened," Julie said slowly.

"Did she complain of any physical pain or aches when you talked to her?" Ms. Dearborn asked.

The three girls were quiet. Julie cocked her head sideways, as if listening to echoes of their talk with Mrs. Babbage.

"I don't remember her mentioning any pains," Julie said.

"She was real worried about that watch," Emily said. "She felt bad about losing it. Really bad."

"But she didn't say anything about being short of breath or having aching joints or anything like that?" Ms. Dearborn asked.

"I don't think so," Julie said. "She said she didn't sleep well last night because she was upset about Mr. Binton."

The woman in the suit stiffened once again. She took a deep breath and looked down at her clipboard.

"Mr. Binton was a dear man and well liked around here," Ms. Dearborn said.

"She said that she was tired," Julie added.

"I see." Ms. Dearborn opened her mouth to say something else but stopped suddenly. She reached under her coat and took out her black beeper. She looked down, reading the message. She frowned. "I'm afraid I'm needed elsewhere." She briskly turned to the young woman who was now sweeping under the bed. "When you're finished, close the room, Maria."

"I will, Ms. Dearborn," the woman said with a slight accent.

"I may need to talk to you all," Ms. Dearborn said to the three girls. "Will you stop by my office later?"

"Sure," Julie said.

"Thank you," the woman said. The girls moved away from the doorway to make room. Julie stepped back and bumped into something hard. She almost lost her balance. She turned around quickly. The man in the wheelchair was right behind them. She had not noticed him roll up behind her. He moved backward out of the way.

"I'm sorry," Julie said.

"My fault," the man said softly.

"Hello, Mr. Carlino," Ms. Dearborn said as she saw the man. She didn't smile.

"Any word on Mrs. Babbage?" he asked as the woman walked by.

"Not yet." The tall woman did not look back at him. She walked quickly down the hall.

"She had a message on her beeper," Julie explained to the man.

"It must have been important," Rebecca said. "She got out of here fast."

"Ms. Dearborn is often in a hurry," the man in the wheelchair said. "She's a very important lady around here."

Julie couldn't tell if he was being serious or not. He rolled past the girls into the room.

"I'm Joe Carlino." The man grinned cheerfully. He quickly looked around the room with his dark, serious eyes. He seemed rather small, sitting in the chair. His arms looked normal, but not strong like some people's that Julie had seen in wheelchairs. His legs looked skinny and limp. He watched Maria sweeping under the bed. "I heard she fell by the bed?"

"She was between the bed and the window," Julie said.

The man rolled over to the bedroom and through the doorway. "Hi, Maria," he said.

"Hello, Mr. Carlino." The woman smiled.

"Maria is well liked around here," the man said to Julie.

"Mr. Carlino!" Maria was obviously pleased by the comment. She blushed.

"It's true," the man continued. "All the residents like Maria. Of course, there are some members of the staff who are not so popular."

"Now, Mr. Carlino, you know what Ms. Dearborn says about criticizing the staff," Maria replied. "She does not like that."

"Well, Maria, you know it's true, and I know it's true, and everyone else knows it's true." The man looked up at Julie and winked. The corners of his mouth turned in a slight grin. "Of course, there's less to criticize since Ms. Dearborn fired several of the staff a few weeks ago. But luckily for all of us, she kept Maria."

"You're teasing me." Maria said pleasantly. She stood up, carefully holding the dustpan full of broken lamp pieces. Mr. Carlino watched her with quick, studious eyes. She dumped the broken pieces into a wastebasket by a night stand. She turned and looked at the man in the wheelchair and the girls.

"I need to get back to Mr. Gorton's room," Maria said. "He asked Ricardo to help him rearrange his room this morning. You know Mr. Gorton. He always gets upset if things aren't done his way, right away."

"Ricardo asked you for help to move furniture?" Mr. Carlino asked.

"Not to help him, but to keep Mr. Gorton from trying to help," Maria said. "Mr. Gorton wants to get up and help him, and he might fall. He's very determined and stubborn for someone ninety-two years old."

"He tells everyone around here that he's got more energy than most seventy-year-old men." The man in the wheelchair smiled broadly. "He's always telling the other residents to quit complaining and act their age."

"Oh." Julie wasn't sure what else to say.

"He will tell you stories for hours until your ears fall off," Maria said. "Of course, everyone is talking about Mr. Binton, and now they'll be talking about Mrs. Babbage. Too many people dying around here."

"Really?" Julie asked curiously.

"I need to go." Maria said. Julie could tell she didn't want to say any more. She looked around the room. "Ms. Dearborn asked me to close the room."

"I can do that," Mr. Carlino offered.

"Are you sure?" Maria looked uncertainly at the children again.

"They are from the church," Mr. Carlino said. "And they're friends of Mrs. Babbage. And you know Mrs. Babbage and I were friends."

"You're friends with everyone, Mr. Carlino," Maria said in a mild rebuke.

"I can lock up for you," the man countered. "Mrs. Babbage asked them to help her find a missing pocket watch. But they didn't get a chance to look in here. We won't take long. They may need my help."

"I guess that's okay," Maria said slowly. "Just make sure the door is shut and locked when you leave. I don't want Ms. Dearborn giving me a bad report. You know how she is with her reports. She's been real worried since Mr. Binton died. And between you and me, I heard there is lots of talk about his death." Mr. Carlino nodded knowingly. Julie saw the look pass between them.

"Really?" Julie asked. "What kind of talk?"

"I shouldn't say," Maria said.

"These children aren't state inspectors, Maria," the man in the wheelchair said. "They're from the church group."

"Well, you know Ms. Dearborn," Maria said to Mr. Carlino. "The inspectors called this morning, but not only that, I heard that the police stopped by too."

"The police?" Mr. Carlino looked surprised.

"They were asking Ms. Dearborn lots of questions, but she won't say anything about it," Maria said. "It's all hush-hush, some kind of big secret. Now Mrs. Babbage is sick. It doesn't look good. Neither of those people was in bad health."

"Did she have heart problems?" Julie asked.

"Not any that I know of," Mr. Carlino said. "And most of the residents around here will tell you in detail every problem in their medical history."

"That's because you're a doctor, Mr. Carlino," Maria said.

"You are?" Julie asked curiously.

"I *was* a doctor, a podiatrist, but I no longer practice medicine, so I make it a point not to advertise the fact that I was a doctor," the man in the wheelchair said quickly. "Being called a doctor in a place like this is almost an open invitation to talk about all kinds of medicine I have no real expertise in. So I avoid it whenever possible. But almost everyone around here talks about their aches and pains and pills to whoever will listen. Mrs. Babbage had problems with arthritis. She was also diabetic. But her heart was in good shape as far as I know."

"She looked good to me the last time I saw her," Maria added. "Of course, you know, sometimes things happen suddenly, like with poor Mr. Binton. He had a pacemaker. Maybe it stopped working. But what do I know? I just clean things up. I don't give out the medicine. I better keep working or I'll get in trouble."

"We won't let you get in trouble," Mr. Carlino said warmly.

"Make sure you lock the door." Maria left the room, carrying her broom and dustpan.

The man watched her go. As soon as she was out of sight, he spun the wheelchair around to face the inside of the apartment. Julie stepped back because she was startled by the suddenness of the movement.

"We should probably hurry." Mr. Carlino looked over his shoulder at the girls. "Ms. Dearborn can appear out of thin air. The staff people are all afraid of her. They act like she can hear through walls and walk through closed doors. Some say she's a ghost. They claim she sneaks up and spies on them. And I have seen her come out of nowhere a few times. So we'd better hurry. I wouldn't want Maria to get in trouble."

"What are you talking about?" Julie asked.

"I came to help you investigate," the man said. "I saw you talking to Mrs. Babbage earlier. You were trying to help her, weren't you?"

"Yes, but—"

"And I'm here to help you." The small man rolled his wheelchair back toward Mrs. Babbage's bedroom. He parked in the doorway of the bedroom and surveyed the room carefully.

"How did you know we were helping Mrs. Babbage?" Julie asked.

"Word gets around quickly in a place like this," Mr. Carlino said. "Besides, I hear and see everything in this place. You can learn a lot if you just sit and listen. I saw you all looking for her watch in the Community Room."

"Do you visit here often?" Emily asked. Like the other girls, she was curious about the small, talkative man in the wheelchair.

"Not at all." The man spun the wheelchair around. "I live here."

"But this is an old folks' home," Rebecca spat out. "You aren't old enough to live here, are you?"

"Rebecca!" Julie moaned.

"Well, he's not old," Rebecca said.

"I'm fifty-one." The man smiled. "But I feel like a man of thirty. Unfortunately, my body won't cooperate." He paused looking down at the wheelchair. He looked up with a half-hearted smile.

"Are you sick?" Rebecca asked. "I mean, how did you hurt your legs?"

"I have multiple sclerosis." Mr. Carlino said. "It's a degenerative nerve disease. I have no close family. My wife left me ten years ago and cleaned me out in the divorce. She didn't want to live the rest of her life with a crippled man."

"That's terrible!" Julie blurted out. She quickly slapped her hand over her mouth. "I'm sorry."

"Don't be," Mr. Carlino mused halfheartedly. Julie felt her heart go out to the little man when she saw the sudden sorrow in his eyes.

"I shouldn't have said that," Julie apologized.

"Really, it's okay," the man said. "Fortunately, we had no children. My wife left and took all the money. She was an Italian and married another Italian, like me. Only he is healthy and a lawyer. I got weaker and weaker. It was too hard to keep practicing medicine, so I just gave that up too. You never know with MS how it will turn out. Some people have it, and it never slows them down much. But that wasn't true for me. It devoured my health. I gave up on just about everything. I used to live in a large city, but I wanted to be in a smaller town. The Manor House is some of the best care available for the money. So that's my little story."

"That's sad," Rebecca said.

"I figured I could be depressed the rest of my life or try to get by." His eyes looked sad. "I had some really awful years. But I'm glad I moved here. But enough about me. Now we need to look around for more clues. I know you detectives are busy people."

The small man in the wheelchair turned it around and rolled into the bedroom. He stopped by the bed.

Julie and the rest of the girls followed him. They watched him carefully.

"We should check the wastebaskets." He rolled over by a wastebasket and looked inside. "They may hold evidence, and we wouldn't want it to get dumped out and lost."

"What evidence?" Julie asked.

"To help with the case." Mr. Carlino peered down into the small metal wastebasket. He reached down, snaking his hand carefully through the broken pieces of lamp.

"But we were helping Mrs. Babbage look for a watch she lost in the Community Room," Emily said. "She wouldn't have thrown it away."

"You can't assume people do rational things when they are upset," the man said. "She may have forgotten what she did last night. But there may be evidence of other things as well."

"Evidence of what things?" Julie asked.

"Perhaps evidence for malpractice." The man in the wheelchair became quiet for a moment. "Or maybe murder." He spun the wheelchair around to face them. His eyes were bright, staring at the children.

"Murder?" Julie asked in shock.

"Possible murder," Mr. Carlino said. "Mrs. Babbage hasn't died. Yet. But she may. Just as Mr. Binton died last night."

"But he had a heart attack," Emily said.

"Maybe it was a heart attack the way they say," the man in the wheelchair mused. "Or maybe it was murder."

A small breeze filled the room. The curtain by the bed blew open. The wind blew harder. The bed covers, which were rumpled and unmade, rustled in the breeze.

"What's that?" Julie walked toward the bed. She pulled back the covers. She reached down between the mattress and bed frame and picked up a tiny plastic syringe with a little sharp needle.

"Yuck, a needle!" Rebecca said.

"Don't touch it!" Mr. Carlino barked out.

Julie dropped the syringe and it fell onto the bed. "I'm sorry. It was between the mattress and the bed frame."

Mr. Carlino rolled over to the edge of the bed. He stared at the needle. He looked around the room quickly. "I think we may have a piece of evidence."

"The needle?" Emily said. "You think someone gave her a shot, like with poison or something?"

"Not poison." Mr. Carlino looked around the room. He rolled over to the nightstand by the bed. He pulled open a drawer. He peered inside. "Just as I thought."

"What?" Julie and the other girls crowded around the wheelchair and looked down into the drawer. They saw combs and a hairbrush, a paperback book, and a tiny box holding about a dozen small glass bottles. An empty glass bottle, about two inches long, lay sideways by itself in the drawer.

"Don't touch anything!" Mr. Carlino whispered.

"Is that some kind of poison?" Rebecca asked.

"It's an insulin vial," the man in the wheelchair replied. "Mrs. Babbage is diabetic. Some people can get better by changing their diets, others by taking pills, and still others need shots. Mrs. Babbage administered her own shots. Insulin is essential to keeping the body chemistry in balance. In a healthy person, your body creates the right amount of sugars. But diabetics need to regulate it by taking insulin."

"Do you think she forgot her shot?" Emily said.

"Not at all," Mr. Carlino said. "The needle on the bed is evidence of that. That's the kind of syringe she used. But she may have taken the wrong dose. Insulin comes in different strengths. If she had the wrong dose, she could go into shock, or into a coma, or even die."

"Wait a minute. When we were looking for her watch, she said she was tired and wanted to come back to her room and take her medicine," Julie said. "Ms. Dearborn just asked if she complained of having pains. I forgot that she mentioned the medicine."

"But why would she take the wrong dose if it's so dangerous?" Rebecca asked.

"She wouldn't if she knew it was wrong," the man said. "That is a new box. Only one bottle has been used. The nursing home provides the medication. We can't touch anything. We've got to notify Ms. Dearborn."

"But the nursing home wouldn't give her the wrong medicine, would they?" Julie asked.

"You wouldn't think so," Mr. Carlino said softly. "But last month another resident, Mrs. Applewhite, died suddenly after going into a coma that could have been caused from insulin shock. She also was diabetic. She did not administer her own shots. The nurses did. No one was sure what happened exactly. She had several health problems besides being diabetic, much worse than Mrs. Babbage. But there was some talk that Mrs. Applewhite died because someone gave her the wrong medicine. The head nurse and two others were fired. The Applewhite family is considering a lawsuit, I hear. It's all very messy. The state inspectors have found other incidents of residents being given improper medications, though none were life-threatening."

"Wow!" Julie's eyes widened.

"I suggest we not touch anything and inform Ms. Dearborn right away," the man said.

Julie and the other girls looked down at the little syringe lying on the bed covers. The wind blew the curtain aside, and the sharp needle glistened as the sun shone on the rumpled bed.

Chapter Five

Clarice's Big Change

Mr. Carlino waited until the girls were in the hallway. He shut the door to Mrs. Babbage's room. He turned the doorknob, making sure it was locked.

"Do you want any help?" Rebecca asked Joe Carlino as he began rolling down the hallway.

"I'm fine." He looked up over his shoulder. "Follow me."

The girls followed the man in the wheelchair down the hallway. Julie felt a rush of confused emotions when she saw Clarice's red hair and Aunt Esther. They were still on the couch. Clarice continued leaning against the old woman's shoulder comfortably. Julie was surprised that Clarice could sit still for so long. The old woman was talking softly as they approached. Julie slowed down.

"I want to talk to her," Julie whispered to Emily and Rebecca.

"You mean about the tiger dream?" Rebecca asked.

"Maybe." Julie's face was uneasy.

The old woman looked up and smiled sweetly as the three girls approached. Joe Carlino slowed his wheelchair to a stop. He watched the three girls curiously.

"Here are your friends now," the old woman said. "You see, they didn't plan to leave you."

"We just stopped to see how you were doing," Julie said. Clarice looked up at the others. Her previous sour and unhappy look was gone.

"You look better," Rebecca said.

"I feel better too," Clarice said softly. "I was pretty scared. I thought Mrs. Babbage had died. I've never seen a dead person."

"You've never been to a funeral?" Rebecca asked.

"Nope," Clarice replied. "I don't think I've ever known anyone who died, like personally."

"What have you been doing?" Julie asked suspiciously.

"We've just been sitting here talking to our heavenly Father," Aunt Esther said warmly. Julie stepped closer. Something was so inviting about the old woman. As she stood closer, she thought she smelled something sweet, like flowers on a spring day. The old woman smiled. Her teeth looked ancient and yellow. A gold filling flashed.

"Yeah, we were actually praying," Clarice said. "Only it wasn't repeating a prayer out of a book or something on a piece of paper. It was really odd."

"How so?" Rebecca asked.

"Because we just sat here and talked to God the way you would talk to a regular person," Clarice said. "I didn't know you could do that with God. I mean, I thought you had to say *thee* and *thou* and stuff like that or say the exact right words or else God wouldn't listen."

"We don't pray with a lot of *thees* and *thous* in our church," Rebecca said. "Sometimes we repeat some prayers but not too often."

"You make it sound like you get kicked off the team if you don't pray right," Julie said to Clarice a bit mockingly.

"Yeah, that's exactly what I mean," Clarice said eagerly. "I thought if you didn't say it right, you failed. Like in school."

"That's not how it works in our church," Emily chided her.

"Well, I don't really know much about how your church does it," Clarice said. "I've only been there a few times."

"Did you pray real formally at other churches?" Emily asked.

"We never went to church," Clarice replied. "The Springdale church is the first church I've gone to, and we've only been there about a month, you know, since we moved here."

"You mean that our church is the first church you've ever attended?" Julie asked in disbelief.

"Yeah," Clarice replied. "Is that okay?"

"You never told us that." Julie sounded suspicious.

"Well, no one ever asked," Clarice replied.

"We all thought you had been to church before," Rebecca said. "I know I did."

"And you've been praying with Aunt Esther?" Julie asked.

"After I stopped crying," Clarice said, "Aunt Esther just asked me if I wanted to pray, and I said I didn't know how. So Aunt Esther said she would show me. She said to tell

God how I felt. So I told him I felt bad about Mrs. Babbage being sick. Actually, I said I felt really scared. And I told him I didn't really want to come to the Manor House and had been mad at my mom about making me come. I told him I was mad at my brother for hiding the remote control on my TV, though now I think maybe I put it somewhere and forgot where I put it. So I'm not mad at him now, I guess."

"You told God all that?" Julie asked.

"That's kind of how I started out," Clarice replied.

"I told her that often we don't know how to pray, but that the Holy Spirit helps us pray." Aunt Esther showed a warm smile.

"Yeah, we talked about the Holy Spirit." Clarice said. "Did you ever hear of the Holy Spirit?"

"Well, of course," Julie said. "The Holy Spirit is God. The Holy Spirit is mentioned all through the Bible."

"But did you know he can live right inside you?" Clarice asked. "That he is called our Helper? Like even if you don't know how to do something, like pray, he will come and help you? Isn't that something? I mean, I can use all the help I can get, especially when it comes to God. I always thought that God was like this big teacher giving you a test, and if you didn't know the answers to the questions, you failed and got kicked out of church and out of heaven. But really, God wants to help us."

"I know that," Julie replied.

"Of course God wants to help us," Emily said. "That's why he gave us Jesus."

"Yeah." Clarice nodded her head. "Aunt Esther was telling me more about Jesus. It's kind of like Jesus takes the test, and we get an A because he passes the test and gives us his A so we're okay with God. It's almost like he cheats, when you think about it. Like God giving us a good grade even when we would have failed and didn't really earn an A."

"I guess that's one way to put it." Emily wore an odd smile. She looked at her friends sideways to see if they were hearing Clarice.

"But did you know that God can make you feel so peaceful?" Clarice asked. "I mean, I never knew God could make you actually *feel* different. As we were sitting here, talking to God about Jesus and all, and the Holy Spirit helping us, I don't know what happened, but I began to feel really peaceful. I don't know when I've ever felt like this before. Did you ever feel God's peace?"

Clarice looked innocently and sincerely at the faces of Julie, Emily and Rebecca. The three girls were surprised to hear a question like that coming out of Clarice's mouth.

"'Be anxious for nothing, but in everything by prayer and supplication with thanksgiving, let your requests be made known unto God,'" Aunt Esther quoted. "'And the peace of God, which passes all understanding, shall keep your hearts and minds through Christ Jesus.' That's found in the book of Philippians, chapter four, verses six and seven."

"That's it exactly!" Clarice said. "It's like having peace but you don't understand it. Did you all ever have that, that peace that passes understanding?"

"I have," Rebecca said.

"Me too," Emily replied.

"Isn't it awesome?" Clarice asked. "I didn't know you could get that, I mean, feeling good and peaceful like that just because you talked to God and told him about your problems. I always thought God was kind of serious and unhappy. Like my dad. I'm going to have to tell my dad about peace that passes understanding. He could really use some of that after his work. He's upset ninety-five percent of the time. He's always worrying about everything and thinks he's behind and failing. He could use an A from Jesus on his test paper."

Julie didn't know what to say. Like her friends, she had experienced God's peace. But she didn't feel peaceful at that moment. And she found it a bit hard to feel glad that Clarice had experienced some of God's peace, even though she knew she should be glad. Julie looked down at the floor. For a moment there was a long pause.

"What did you tell the Father about your friends?" Aunt Esther asked.

"Well, I told God that I was afraid you were going to ignore me the rest of the day and not invite me to be with you." Clarice looked down at her hands. "I told him I didn't think you all liked me. But I told him that I didn't blame you, since I accused you of taking my CD player. I told him I was sorry about saying that.

"And then Aunt Esther said I should say that I was sorry to you. So I am saying that. I'm sorry I accused you of taking my CD player. I shouldn't have done it. I forgot where I put it. And I just thought you were trying to be mean. In my old school, right before we moved to Springdale, some kids in my classroom really did steal my old CD player. They were real mean about it. I thought it was happening all over again. Anyway, I'm sorry I accused you guys and all."

"That's okay, Clarice. We forgive you," Emily said.

"Our attitude hasn't been good toward you either," Rebecca said. "So we're sorry for that. And I'm glad you're getting to know God better. And I'm glad you've started coming to our church, and I'm actually glad you came here today."

"God is really awesome," Clarice said. "I never knew God really liked me."

Julie looked at Clarice. The girl with pale skin and stringy red hair now had a beautiful smile on her face. It was a new expression for Clarice.

"We were going to see Ms. Dearborn, the Manor House manager," Julie said in an even voice. "You're welcome to come with us if you'd like, Clarice."

"I'll come along later if that's okay," Clarice said. "I want to hang out some more with Aunt Esther, if that's okay."

"Are you sure?" Rebecca asked. "You can come with us if you want, like Julie said."

"That's okay. Maybe I will later," Clarice said. "This is more fun. I never thought that talking to God could be fun and make you feel good."

"Clarice is getting to know our Father," the old woman said.

"Could I maybe talk to you later?" Julie asked the old woman.

"Well, of course, Julie," Aunt Esther said. "I've been wanting to talk to you too."

"Really?" Julie suddenly felt special that the woman even knew her name. She turned to Clarice. "We'd better go now."

"I'll catch up with you later," Clarice said. "Tell my

mom where I am if you see her."

"Okay." Julie nodded.

"Follow me, ladies." Joe Carlino rolled his chair forward. The three girls followed him. They were in the middle of the Community Room when Rebecca stopped. The man in the wheelchair stopped too.

"Isn't that something about Clarice?" Rebecca whispered to the other girls.

"I think it's really good," Emily said. "I think we kind of judged her too quickly, if you know what I mean."

"It sounds like she became a Christian while sitting in the hallway with Aunt Esther." Julie shook her head.

"It sounds like that to me too," Rebecca added. "I just assumed she was a Christian because they started coming to our church. But maybe today is the day she really met God."

"She really did look peaceful too," Rebecca said. "I think she has experienced God's love. No one could fake an expression like that."

"She seemed to be telling the truth to me," Emily said. "What do you think, Julie?"

"I think that Aunt Esther must really know how to pray," Julie said. "She seems like a really unusual woman to me. Kind of odd."

"She's a character all right," Joe Carlino said.

"Do you know her very well?" Emily asked.

"I've never met anyone like her," Mr. Carlino said. "She has more genuine faith in God than anyone I've ever seen. She used to be a missionary in China, I heard. One time I sneaked up on her while she was praying. I came right up behind her so she couldn't see me, and I know she didn't hear me. I felt like I was eavesdropping on a private conversation between two people in love. I was embarrassed and ashamed. That woman talks to God like no one I've ever heard.

"She had her eyes shut tight, but I'm telling you, I hadn't been listening for more than two minutes when she began praying about me and my disease and my ex-wife. She prayed about things I had never mentioned to anyone. It was like she was reading my journal or opening my mail. It was spooky. She couldn't have known I was behind her."

"Maybe God *was* sitting beside her and told her about you," Julie grunted uncomfortably.

"I wondered about that myself," Mr. Carlino said. "I was raised a Catholic but haven't been very religious for several years. I've been afraid to say anything to her because I was acting a little devious, and I shouldn't have been doing that."

"I don't think she'd care," Rebecca said. "She just kind of oozes love, if you ask me."

"That's a good way to put it," Emily agreed. "She is very unusual."

The three girls continued walking across the Community Room. Joe Carlino rolled himself along in front of them. When they reached the Recreation Room, it was full of people painting, knitting and doing needlework. Several women were gathered around a huge quilting frame, sewing and talking.

Mrs. Morgan waved when she saw Julie.

"I was just about to go look for you," Mrs. Brown said. "I heard all about Mrs. Babbage, poor thing. I would have gone to her room, but Ms. Dearborn asked the ladies from the church to keep as many of the residents occupied as possible and out of that hallway. Have you heard any news about her condition?"

"Not yet," Julie said softly. "She looked really sick. But there may be more going on than we first thought."

"What do you mean?" Mrs. Brown asked. Julie pulled her mother aside. The other girls and Mr. Carlino followed. Julie quickly introduced her mother to the man in the wheelchair. Then she began telling her mother everything that had happened. Mrs. Brown looked surprised and then concerned.

"So now we're looking for Ms. Dearborn," Julie said. "Mr. Carlino thinks it's possible she took the wrong medicine or the wrong amount."

"Well, I've heard the story about Mrs. Applewhite," Mrs. Brown said. "Her family is pursuing a lawsuit against the Manor House. I also heard that the police were here asking questions about Mr. Binton. You girls are having quite a day. Where's Clarice? You're being nice to her, aren't you?"

"She's with that older lady they call Aunt Esther," Rebecca said. "And you should see them. We think Clarice became a Christian this morning."

"That's wonderful!" Mrs. Brown said.

"You should see her and Aunt Esther," Emily added. "They have been sitting on a couch, praying."

"I don't doubt it." Mrs. Brown laughed. "Aunt Esther is famous for her prayers."

"Do you know her?" Julie asked.

"I've talked with her and prayed with her several times," her mother said. "She's a very devout woman. She and her husband were missionaries in China. Her husband was put in jail and then killed by the Communists. Aunt Esther spent time in jail herself. I've heard some of the ladies say she displays remarkable spiritual gifts. Everyone says that she is a prayer warrior. She's over a hundred years old. She's very loving and very much like Jesus."

"I think she's kind of strange," Julie said. "Are you sure she's okay?"

"Of course she's okay," Mrs. Brown said. "She's a bit different, but I know she has a very deep relationship with God. I'm glad she and Clarice are getting to spend some time together. I've never known Clarice to go out of her way to pray."

"Me either," Julie said. "They're like big pals, practically." Once again, unpleasant feelings churned inside her stomach. Julie didn't want to admit it, but she felt angry at Clarice, and she wasn't sure why.

"Are you feeling okay?" Mrs. Brown looked carefully at her daughter's face.

"I don't know," Julie muttered. Her face fell. She wasn't sure what to say.

"It must have been quite upsetting to find Mrs. Babbage," her mother said.

"Yeah, I guess." But Julie knew that wasn't it, even though it did bother her. She didn't know if she wanted to talk to her mother about what she was really feeling. But wanting to hide the ugly feelings made them churn even harder in her stomach.

"Have you girls eaten lunch?" Mrs. Brown asked.

"Not yet," Julie said.

"There are sandwiches on the side table and soft drinks," Mrs. Brown said. "I want you to eat right now. It's already twelve o'clock."

"Okay," Julie said. "I lost track of time. We'd better make it fast. I think it's important to talk to Ms. Dearborn."

Mr. Carlino joined the three girls while they hurriedly took time out for ham and cheese sandwiches, corn chips and icy cold sodas. They finished eating, and Julie went back to see her mother.

"We're doing fine here," Mrs. Brown said. "We've got plenty of projects going, and I think it's best for everyone if we just keep going until things settle down."

"Let's find Ms. Dearborn then," Julie said.

"Her office is down that hall." Mr. Carlino pointed across the room. The three girls followed him. He moved more quickly than they expected through the crowded recreation room.

The door to Ms. Dearborn's office was closed. Her secretary looked suspiciously at Mr. Carlino and the three girls.

"Hi, Samantha," Mr. Carlino said cheerfully. "We need to see Ms. Dearborn right away."

"She's busy, Mr. Carlino," the secretary said firmly.

"But this is really important," Rebecca said. "We have news about Mrs. Babbage."

"She's with someone right now," the secretary replied.

"But this could be *really* important," Emily pleaded. "Maybe life or death—or even murder."

The secretary raised her eyebrows at the mention of murder. She reached for the phone, but the door to Ms. Dearborn's office opened suddenly. Ms. Dearborn walked out briskly, followed by a man in a suit and a policeman. When she saw the three girls and Mr. Carlino, she paused.

"We have some news about Mrs. Babbage that we think

you may need to check into," Mr. Carlino said.

"Yeah, we found a needle stuck down in the side of her bed frame," Rebecca blurted out. "Julie actually found it. But Mr. Carlino thinks it might be important. And he's a doctor."

"He's not a practicing doctor," Ms. Dearborn said evenly. She did not look pleased to hear any more news or surprises. The two men with her, however, looked very interested. "Actually, we were just on our way to the hospital to check on Mrs. Babbage."

"I'd like to hear what you have to say," the man in the suit said seriously. "I'm from the state health office. My name is Sam Boone. This is Officer Franklin."

"Let's talk before we leave," the policeman said. "This may have some bearing on our investigation."

"We heard you were investigating." Rebecca sounded excited. "We've been investigating this morning too."

"Actually, we were just trying to help Mrs. Babbage look for a lost watch," Julie said. "But then she got sick. And while we were in her room we found the needle and just wondered about some things."

"Are you sure we have time for this now?" Ms. Dearborn asked impatiently. "The needle you found was probably left by the emergency crew. Those hospital crews are busy and careless at times. We've had problems with them before."

"Given the recent problems and questions regarding the quality of care in the Manor House, I would think you would want to know more about these issues than we do," Mr. Boone said seriously. "Unless you feel that your staff has something to hide."

"I can assure you that is not the issue." Ms. Dearborn's

cheeks flushed red. "I just assumed we were wanted over at the hospital right away. Sergeant Haskins seemed urgent on the telephone."

"I can explain everything to Sergeant Haskins," the policeman said.

"Then let's see what these young people found," Inspector Boone replied.

The girls introduced themselves as they led the way to Mrs. Babbage's room. Joe Carlino and Julie brought up the rear.

"Ms. Dearborn is really steamed," he said softly to Julie.

Clarice and Aunt Esther were still sitting on the couch in the hallway. Clarice had her eyes closed, and she was talking softly. Julie could tell she was praying without actually hearing the words. The group passed by without disturbing them.

Ms. Dearborn took out her keys and opened Mrs. Babbage's door. Mr. Boone and Officer Franklin walked in first, followed by Ms. Dearborn. Julie was the last one inside.

The bedroom was crowded with so many people gathered around the bed. When Julie walked up, everyone was quiet.

"The needle is gone," Rebecca said loudly. "It was right there."

"The medicine bottles are gone too," Emily said. "Everything's gone."

Chapter Six

Mrs. Barclay's Strange Answer

"We didn't move the needle or the medicine," Julie said. "Who would have taken them?"

"That's what I would like to know." The inspector frowned, raised his eyebrows and then looked at Ms. Dearborn.

"I don't know anything about it," she said quickly. "I never saw the syringe the children are talking about, and I never looked in the nightstand drawer. Mrs. Babbage was diabetic, and she gave herself insulin shots."

"But the Manor House supplied the insulin?"

"I would assume she got it from our staff, yes," Ms. Dearborn said.

"Who has keys to this room other than Mrs. Babbage?"

"Well, the only people I know for sure are the staff, unless she gave a key to someone else, like one of her daughters," Ms. Dearborn said.

Officer Franklin took a cell phone off his belt. He punched in some numbers and walked out of the bedroom. He talked softly inside the small kitchen area. Julie tried to hear but couldn't.

"When did you last see the needle and vial here?"

"It was around 11:30, I suppose." Joe Carlino looked at his watch.

"Are any of your staff scheduled for rounds this time of day?" Officer Haskins asked.

"Not that I know of." Ms. Dearborn's face was filled with discouragement. "Maria was in here earlier and helped clean up. She may have taken them."

"We actually left after Maria left." Mr. Carlino looked uneasy. "I told her it would be all right."

"You told her it would be all right?" Ms. Dearborn asked coldly.

"We didn't stay long," Mr. Carlino replied. "Mrs. Babbage had asked the girls to look for the watch, and we thought it might be in the room."

"It might be a good idea to talk to this aide, Maria," the inspector said. "I can understand someone throwing away a used syringe, in a proper container of course. But I don't understand why someone would remove unused bottles of insulin. Do you, Ms. Dearborn?"

"That does seem irregular," Ms. Dearborn replied. "I will call Maria."

"Last I heard, she was helping Ricardo in Mr. Gorton's room," Mr. Carlino said.

Ms. Dearborn looked very unhappy. She picked up the telephone by the bed and asked her secretary to find Maria.

"Maybe Clarice and Aunt Esther saw something," Julie

offered. "They've been sitting out in the hallway all this time."

"That's right!" Rebecca replied. "I bet they saw anyone who came into this room."

"Let's hope so," Ms. Dearborn said.

Julie ran out into the hallway and rushed down to the couch. Clarice and the old woman were still talking.

"Clarice, Clarice!" Julie was breathless. "We need your help. We need to know if you saw anyone come down this hall since we talked to you last."

"I don't know," Clarice said. "I wasn't really paying attention."

"But it's important," Rebecca added.

"Yeah, Clarice," Emily agreed. Clarice was surprised to see Ms. Dearborn, Mr. Boone and Officer Franklin looking at her.

"Did you see anyone?" Ms. Dearborn asked Aunt Esther.

"Well now, I need to think," the old woman said. "I saw these children. But then I was praying and had my eyes closed for a long time."

"Me too," Clarice said. "I was praying with her. I had my eyes closed too."

Just then Maria came down the hallway. Officer Franklin pulled her to one side and began talking softly to her. Ms. Dearborn started to walk over, but she caught Officer Franklin's warning glance and stopped.

"Wait a minute," Clarice said. "I think I did see someone."

"Who was it?" Julie asked.

"I don't know," Clarice said. "I heard a rattle and an odd squishing kind of sound. I opened my eyes. The rattle was one of those carts they have around here with medicine and things on it."

"A nurse's cart?" Ms. Dearborn asked.

"Yeah," Clarice said. "But I didn't see a face. Whoever it was wore a white coat. I don't remember anything else."

"You didn't see her face?"

"I'm not sure it was even a woman," Clarice said. "I guess I assumed it was a woman."

"What was the squishing sound?" Julie asked.

"I don't know," Clarice said. "I mean, I didn't think about it. I just saw someone pushing a cart, and I closed my eyes again because we were praying. I think I may have heard a door open or shut. Wait a second. I did open my eyes later. I saw the person down at the end of the hall."

"By Mrs. Babbage's room?" Ms. Dearborn asked.

"No, it was farther down than that," Clarice said. "It was way down at the end of the hall. I saw the person push the cart into the last room. Now I remember."

"Did the person come back?" Julie asked.

"I don't think so," Clarice said. "And we've been sitting here the whole time."

Officer Franklin walked over. His face was pleasant but serious.

"Maria says she did not return to Mrs. Babbage's room," the policeman said.

"Someone may be down at the end of the hallway," Julie said. "Clarice said she saw a nurse pushing a cart down there."

"I don't know that it was a nurse for sure," Clarice said.

"Let's go look in the last room," Rebecca said.

"Sounds like a plan," Officer Franklin said. "Who's in

that room?"

"Mrs. Barclay." Ms. Dearborn began walking. Everyone except the children and Aunt Esther followed her.

"Is it okay if I come?" Clarice asked Julie. "Aunt Esther and I are done praying."

"Well, I guess so." Julie sounded reluctant. "I mean, sure. You are the star witness here."

"I'll talk to you later, Aunt Esther," Clarice said to the old woman.

"I'll be praying that you children uncover what's hidden and find everything that's missing." The old woman stood slowly to her feet.

Julie and the three other girls ran to catch up. A door was at the very end of hallway, but it was covered by an emergency bar.

"This hall door won't open without setting off the fire alarm," Ms. Dearborn pointed out to the others. Then she turned to the last room. She fitted her key in the lock. She knocked on the door as she turned the knob.

"Mrs. Barclay!" she said loudly as she opened the door. The children were the last ones inside. It reminded Julie of a hospital room.

Ms. Dearborn stared at a nurse's cart in the center of the room. On the top of the cart, lying on a white towel, was a tiny plastic syringe.

"That looks just like the one we found, doesn't it?" Julie asked.

"It's the same kind." Mr. Carlino nodded.

A very old woman was on her side in a high hospital bed. She had straps around her waist. Her sunken eyes looked out with a blank expression. A breeze blew through the window.

Officer Franklin walked over.

"The screen is missing," he said. "It looks like whoever brought that cart in here opened this window to get out. Mrs. Barclay must have seen the whole thing."

"She has Alzheimer's disease," Ms. Dearborn said with a very tired voice. She looked at the open window and then sat down. "She is in the advanced stages of the disease with severe dementia. She wouldn't know her own husband or her children, unfortunately."

"This is like a setup," Julie said.

"What do you mean?" Rebecca asked.

"I mean it just seems like someone left this cart and needle on purpose," Julie replied. "That needle looks like it's waiting to be found. But the person took the insulin bottles."

"That's a possibility," Officer Franklin said. "Or whoever left it could have been in a hurry and forgot the needle but not the insulin."

"You aren't even going to ask Mrs. Barclay?" Clarice asked.

"It wouldn't do any good," Rebecca whispered. "She's got Alzheimer's."

"Mrs. Barclay, Mrs. Barclay!" Ms. Dearborn called out loudly, leaning down next to the woman on the bed. Mrs. Barclay's eyes blinked. She swallowed several times. "Did you see who came into your room, Mrs. Barclay?"

"Water. Water," the old woman croaked out in a whisper.

"Did you see who brought in this cart, Mrs. Barclay?"

"Water," the old woman repeated.

"She's not going to be any help." Ms. Dearborn lifted a

small plastic water glass off a nearby bed table and held a straw up to the old woman's lips, but she wouldn't drink. Her eyes looked forward but didn't seem to focus.

"She'll drink when she really gets thirsty," Ms. Dearborn said.

"That's so sad." Clarice looked at the old woman.

Officer Franklin took the cell phone off his belt and stepped into the hallway.

"I'm sorry you're having such a bad day," Clarice said softly to Ms. Dearborn. "You look really tired."

"I am." The tall woman rubbed her face with her hands. "We were up most of the night with Mr. Binton, and now one thing after another is going wrong. This has been a very long day."

"I'm sorry too, Karen," Mr. Carlino said to the manager. "And I apologize if I usurped your authority with Maria. That wasn't right. I assured Maria that it was okay, and I can be very persuasive."

"I realize you have your charms with my staff, Mr. Carlino," Ms. Dearborn acknowledged. "I wish I got along with them as well. I just hope we can get to the bottom of this." She stared with tired eyes at the abandoned nurse's cart. Officer Franklin returned.

"Sergeant Haskins says to seal off this room," the tall policeman said. "He'll send someone over to check for fingerprints around the window."

"They won't find them," Mr. Carlino said.

"Why not?"

"Because this cart has a half-used box of latex gloves right there," the man in the wheelchair said. "Whoever did this is smart enough to use gloves."

"You're probably right, but we still need to check," the officer said. "Sergeant Haskins would also like us to meet him over at the hospital."

"What about us?" Julie asked.

"He wants to talk to all of you too," the officer said. "And Mr. Carlino as well."

The children filed out of the room. Clarice stayed by Mrs. Barclay's bed.

"Mrs. Barclay, wake up!" Clarice said loudly. "We need your help."

"Come on, Clarice," Julie called out, but the red-haired girl had her head bent down low beside the old woman. "Clarice, we have to go!" Julie called louder. "They're waiting for us."

"Maria can stay here until your men arrive," Ms. Dearborn said.

"We can ask if anyone saw a person come out of this window," Officer Franklin said. "But since it's on the end at the back of the building, I don't think we'll get much of a response. Whoever did this knew what they were doing."

"Mrs. Barclay, did you see anyone?" Clarice asked once more. She listened and then offered the old woman her glass of water, but the woman acted as if she didn't want a drink yet.

"We're leaving, Clarice!" Julie said.

Clarice shook her head sadly. She joined the others outside.

"She wouldn't take any water from me either," Clarice said. "I can't believe the police want to ask us questions."

"I just wish we had some good answers," Julie said. Both girls ran down the long hallway to catch up with the others.

Chapter Seven

Julie's Elementary Deduction

The children told their mothers they were needed at the hospital. Mrs. Brown did not seem surprised. She knew Sergeant Haskins because he was a member of their church.

They went in two cars across the street to the hospital. Clarice was especially excited, but not about the mysteries in the nursing home. Instead it was the mysteries of God that had her attention.

"God is hard to figure out," Clarice said. "All these years I thought he was kind of boring and mean, but really God isn't like that at all. And I thought prayer was boring too. But when I prayed with Aunt Esther it was fun. It was like flying a kite."

"What?" Julie asked.

"That's what it reminded me of," Clarice said. "I was praying with Aunt Esther after you all left, and it was really neat. I was talking, and it was like letting loose a beautiful kite on a breezy day. You know how that feels? You let go of the kite and the wind catches it and pulls it out of your hand so fast that the ball of string almost burns your fingers? My words felt like a kite in the wind. As soon as they were out of my mouth, it was like some wonderful wind grabbed them and pulled them all the way up to heaven. And a whole string of words kept coming out, just like a kite string being pulled out of your hand. Only these words felt as if they were pulled out of my heart. It was really neat because the words came so easy and fast. I could hardly believe what I was saying. It felt wonderful. I never prayed like that in my life."

"That's a neat way to put it," Rebecca said. "I've felt kind of like that sometimes when I pray, but not very often."

"Aunt Esther says the Holy Spirit makes your prayers soar like the wind," Clarice said. "I never heard anyone talk the way she does."

The police car pulled into the hospital parking lot. The girls got out and waited while Mr. Carlino got into his wheelchair.

Inside, the hospital was busy. Sergeant Haskins smiled broadly when he saw Julie and her friends.

"How did you all get drawn into this?" Sergeant Haskins asked.

"We were looking for Mrs. Babbage's lost watch," Julie said. "We didn't find her watch, but we found other things."

"You did make a difference with Mrs. Babbage," the officer said. "If you hadn't found her so quickly, she could have died."

"It was Clarice that went to her room first," said Emily.

"Is she all right?" Clarice asked hopefully.

"No," the officer replied. "The ER people moved her to intensive care. She seems to be in a coma."

"Oh, no!" Clarice said.

"Did they check for insulin problems?" Mr. Carlino asked.

"Yes," the sergeant replied. "And from what they said, an insulin overdose could be the trouble. Her symptoms look like a diabetic coma, which is why I'm interested in your account of what's been going on at the Manor House. So why don't you all give me an update?"

Taking turns, Julie and the others, including Mr. Carlino, went over the whole story, each adding anything he or she thought was relevant. Clarice listened carefully, since she had missed out on most of the activities while sitting with Aunt Esther.

"So you found the abandoned nurse's cart in Mrs. Barclay's room, and she is too senile to help us out," Sergeant Haskins repeated.

"That's right," Julie said. "And I think whoever left it there left the needle on purpose."

"That's possible," Sergeant Haskins said. "But why would they go to that much trouble? Why not leave it in Mrs. Babbage's room?"

"Because . . . because . . ." Julie said, thinking. "I don't know. I just think it has to be on purpose. It just 'looked' like it was left deliberately."

"But they didn't leave the insulin bottles," the sergeant said. "Why would they leave the needle but take the insulin?"

"Maybe it was more important to keep the insulin bottles so no one would find out they were the wrong dose,"

Clarice said. "I mean, if someone made a mistake, they would try to hide it."

"That's what Mr. Boone thinks is very likely," Sergeant Haskins said. "And I'm inclined to think that's a very good possibility myself."

"So you think someone on the nursing-home staff gave Mrs. Babbage the wrong medicine?" Julie asked.

"They may have even done the same with Mr. Binton," Sergeant Haskins added.

"I thought he died of a heart attack," Rebecca asked. "Did he get bad heart medicine?"

"Insulin is the suspected problem in Mr. Binton's death as well," the officer said.

"Really?" Julie asked.

"Mr. Binton was also a diabetic." Mr. Carlino raised his eyebrows. "I forgot about that. An overdose of insulin could cause a heart attack, especially in someone with a history of heart problems."

"You mean they both took the wrong amount of insulin?" Julie said. "What a strange coincidence!"

"It may not be a coincidence," Sergeant Haskins replied slowly.

"You mean it may have been intentional?" Julie asked. "Then that would mean he was murdered!"

"That's what it would mean." The sergeant nodded his head. "And it could be attempted murder of Mrs. Babbage if that theory is correct."

"But why would someone want to murder Mr. Binton?" Rebecca asked.

"Or Mrs. Babbage?" Clarice asked. "She was real nice."

"Well, we have to consider all possibilities in an

investigation," Sergeant Haskins said. "We don't want to jump to conclusions without more facts. But when someone dies under suspicious circumstances, we try to rule out homicide first and then move on. We have to consider all the possibilities, and murder is one possibility. Negligence is another possibility, and probably more likely."

"You mean the Manor House may be responsible for giving the wrong dosage of medicine?" Julie asked.

"They administer the medicine," the officer replied. "So they are legally responsible."

"I would have thought that after Mrs. Applewhite's case the nursing staff would have taken extra precautions, especially in giving out insulin." Mr. Carlino shook his head. "That is gross negligence if they made mistakes like that three times."

"Mr. Boone, the state health inspector, agrees with you," Sergeant Haskins said. "The Applewhites will have a stronger case if they can prove neglect in other cases. Mr. Binton's family has already talked to a lawyer, I hear. And I imagine Mrs. Babbage's family will also consider a lawsuit if Mrs. Babbage was given a wrong dose of medicine."

"But I thought Ms. Dearborn fired the staff people she thought had caused the problems," Julie said.

"She did dismiss three staff," Sergeant Haskins said. "All three of the terminated nurses denied any negligence. Nothing was ever proven, but there were lots of accusations flying around. Two of the nurses work here at the hospital now. They have considered suing the Manor House because they feel they were fired unfairly. And as you may have heard, the hospital nurses and the Manor House staff have also had disagreements over sharing health care and expenses for Manor House residents. That's another can of worms."

"What a mess," Julie said. "No one can prove anything, and everyone is suing everybody. And somebody at the Manor House is giving out bad medicine."

"Well, finding that abandoned cart and knowing that those insulin vials were stolen is solid evidence that someone is hiding something," Sergeant Haskins said. "You kids have been a real help."

"So you think someone at the Manor House is still giving out the wrong medicine to people and trying to cover their mistakes?" Rebecca asked.

"That's a possibility," the officer replied.

"I wonder who it is," Clarice said. "It's kind of spooky thinking someone might give you bad medicine."

"That's why Ms. Dearborn is so upset," Mr. Carlino said. "You can't lose credibility like that and stay open for business."

"It also means the three nurses Ms. Dearborn fired were innocent," Julie said. "No wonder they were angry."

"I know Mrs. Pierce was extremely upset," Mr. Carlino said. "As head of the staff, she had her reputation on the line. If this investigation plays out the way it seems headed right now, she will have a strong case if she sues."

"I wouldn't want to be Ms. Dearborn with everyone suing me," Julie said. "No wonder she looks so discouraged."

"But it's not her fault, directly," Rebecca said. "It doesn't seem right. She didn't give out the wrong medicine. It was the people who worked for her. Will she get in trouble herself, or will it be the Manor House?"

"The Manor House is owned by a corporation that owns several eldercare facilities in five states," the officer said. "They have malpractice insurance, I'm sure. None of the pending lawsuits have actually been filed yet because there is an ongoing investigation."

"Why did you mention murder?" Mr. Carlino had a curious look in his eye. "Negligence isn't considered murder."

"I said we try to rule out murder when there are suspicions around a death," the sergeant said. "When you think about murder, you have to consider a motive. You have to ask who would benefit if someone dies of seemingly natural causes. The usual motive is money."

"Family members are suspects, because they can collect life insurance and get an inheritance, right?" Clarice asked eagerly.

"That's often the case," the officer replied. "For instance, in the Binton family, it is public knowledge that Mr. Binton and his sons disagreed about the family jewelry business. The two sons, Roger and John, have been seen in public arguing with their father about the family business and money problems."

"It sounds like you've been investigating the Bintons," Mr. Carlino observed, raising his eyebrows.

"Well, I don't want to divulge too much," the officer said. "But we have interviewed several people around town and in the Manor House regarding the Bintons on some troubling questions about their business deals. In fact, I'm waiting for a phone call with some important information. We may be talking to his sons again very soon."

"I would like to talk to Mr. Binton's sons myself," Julie said.

"Why is that?" Sergeant Haskins asked.

"Because of Mrs. Babbage's watch," Julie said. "I've been thinking about it all morning. Mr. Binton was trying to fix it last night. And then he fell over with a heart attack. Mrs. Babbage was upset and lost track of the watch. We looked everywhere around where they were sitting and didn't find it. But then it occurred to me when we came into the hospital that the emergency crew might have seen the watch lying there on the floor and assumed it belonged to Mr. Binton. It was a man's watch, not a woman's watch."

"So you think they put the pocket watch into Mr. Binton's pocket," Clarice said with admiration. "You *are* a detective. I should have thought of that."

"That's a good possibility," Sergeant Haskins said. "And I know an easy way to find out. Mr. Binton's body is in the hospital morgue. Whatever clothes and personal belongings he had on him when he came to the hospital will still be here."

"Can we look now?"

"Let me make a phone call first." The sergeant took a cell phone off his belt. He walked out of earshot of the three girls and Mr. Carlino.

"What happened to Ms. Dearborn and the others?" Julie asked.

"I think they went to ICU to talk with Mrs. Babbage's family," Mr. Carlino said. "I think her oldest daughter is here."

"What a day this has turned out to be!" Julie said.

"No kidding," Clarice added. "I wanted to stay home and watch TV, but today has been one of the best days of my life. Things are turning out way differently than I expected."

"I think we may have found your missing watch," Sergeant Haskins said as he returned. He stuck the cell phone back on his black belt, not far from his holstered revolver. "We'll meet Detective Ortiz down in the morgue. Both Roger and John Binton are there making arrangements for their father's body. Detective Ortiz, who has been investigating the case, says he saw a pocket watch earlier in Mr. Binton's belongings."

"It sounds like you have them under surveillance." Mr. Carlino rolled his wheelchair beside the police officer.

"Well, we have been keeping a watch." The officer walked into the elevator. "And you'll understand why in just a few moments."

"We won't have to look at any dead bodies in the morgue, will we?" Rebecca slowed down as they came upon the two swinging doors that said *Morgue* in red letters.

"Not at all," Officer Haskins said. "We'll just be in the outer office. Mr. Binton's clothes and belongings will be in a box."

The air in the morgue was colder than the other rooms, Julie thought, as they passed the swinging doors. Or maybe she felt colder, knowing she was close to where the hospital kept dead people.

Three men in suits were standing in front of a desk. Police Officer Franklin entered the morgue office right behind Sergeant Haskins.

The three men at the desk turned around when they heard footsteps. Julie could tell right away who the Binton sons were because they both had thinning blond hair and looked alike. The other man was Detective Ortiz, she assumed.

An older woman sat behind the desk, chewing on the end of her pencil. A file folder and box were on her desk. The two Binton sons looked tired and angry.

"Finally we can get moving on this thing," the taller son said.

"Hi, Roger," Officer Haskins said in a businesslike tone. He quickly introduced the children and Joe Carlino and explained why they had come down to the morgue.

"We'd like to go through your father's belongings to look for the watch," Sergeant Haskins said.

"Sure, anything to get this show on the road," Roger Binton said impatiently. "We've been waiting to move my father's body all morning. I don't understand why there is such a delay."

"We'll get to that in a moment," the officer said.

The woman behind the desk picked up a cardboard box and set it on her desk. She took the lid off the box and nodded for Julie to take a look.

Julie looked inside. There were clothes inside a large sealed plastic bag. In another bag was a ring, a wristwatch and a large round pocket watch.

"I think that's it!" Julie said excitedly. "Can I take it out of the bag?"

"I'll do it for you." The woman put on a pair of gloves, carefully opened the bag, picked up the gold pocket watch, and held it out to Julie. The watch was heavier than she expected. She opened the case. Engraved inside the lid was the list of names and dates that Mrs. Babbage had described.

"This is Mrs. Babbage's watch!" Julie said. "See the names and dates!"

She held the watch up for the others to see. The two Binton sons looked mildly surprised. Roger Binton once again looked impatiently at Sergeant Haskins.

"You did it!" Clarice said. "You found her watch!"

Julie smiled.

Chapter Eight

Sarah's Birth Date

"It was just a guess." Julie looked at the watch. "And the process of elimination. Can we give this to Mrs. Babbage? I mean, when she wakes up?"

"I'm sure she'll want it," Sergeant Haskins said.

"Can we finish the paperwork now?" Roger Binton asked impatiently. "We've had a very trying day, and we still have many things to do and business matters to attend to."

"We have one other matter to discuss." Sergeant Haskins pulled papers out of his pocket. "We have search warrants to look inside your briefcases."

"What?" Roger Binton asked.

"You should also know we have search warrants for your automobile as well as for your homes and place of business," Detective Ortiz said.

"Search warrants?" The younger brother wore a puzzled expression.

"What's going on here?" Roger Binton demanded. He began reading the search warrant.

"We'd like you to open your briefcases now, please," Sergeant Haskins said. "We can open them by force if necessary."

"That isn't necessary." Roger Binton angrily picked up his briefcase and set it on the desk. He spun the numbers on the combination lock and snapped the lid open. "Please be careful. I have a laptop computer in there."

Detective Ortiz immediately began searching inside the black briefcase. He lifted the laptop computer out carefully while Roger Binton watched, frowning.

"We need to have both briefcases open," Sergeant Haskins said to John Binton.

"Sure." The younger Binton put his briefcase on a chair. "The lock hasn't worked for over a year, so you can open it."

Sergeant Haskins snapped open the lid. He lifted out files and papers. He pulled back the zipper on a pouch connected to the lid. He looked inside and then paused.

"What's wrong?" John Binton asked.

"Are you diabetic?" Sergeant Haskins asked.

"No, of course not," John answered.

"Then why do you have these?" Sergeant Haskins pulled open the pocket wider. Inside were several small glass insulin bottles. Next to them were several needles. One vial had been opened and apparently used.

"I don't know where those came from!" John Binton's face was filled with confusion. None of the police officers said a word. "My father was a diabetic, but I sure didn't put those there! I never touched his medicine."

The air in the morgue seemed suddenly colder as everyone looked at the glass bottles and the small, sharp needles.

"You'd all better go now," Sergeant Haskins said to Julie and the others. "We have some matters we need to discuss with the Bintons."

The four girls and the man in the wheelchair left the morgue after Julie signed a paper saying she had taken the watch. Julie didn't mention it, but she was relieved to be out of the cold, creepy room. In her hand she carried Mrs. Babbage's gold pocket watch.

"Do you believe it?" Clarice said as they walked out of the morgue. "He's in there reading them their Miranda rights, just like on TV!"

"I've heard the police do that before in other cases we've been on," Julie said.

"Really?" Clarice was clearly impressed.

"A few times, actually," Julie said.

"Did you see the look on his face when they found those bottles of insulin?" Rebecca asked.

"Do you think they committed murder, Mr. Carlino?" Julie asked.

"It looks very suspicious," the man in the wheelchair said. "He said they had been investigating them and had several other search warrants. He must have some evidence of criminal activity, because you can't get a search warrant without some solid evidence."

"Finding those needles and that insulin in his briefcase was bad enough," Emily said. "He really looked guilty."

"Do you think so?" Julie asked. "I thought he looked honestly surprised. I mean, maybe he's being framed.

That's what I heard him say as we were leaving."

"His brother didn't look surprised," Rebecca said.

"Maybe his brother is framing him," Clarice said. "They said they were fighting over the family business. I thought he looked surprised too."

"Do you know them?" Julie asked the former doctor.

"I would see them around the Manor House," Mr. Carlino said. "They would visit their father regularly. And I did hear them argue a few times. One time I heard Roger and his father criticizing John over business decisions and his love life."

"His love life?" Clarice asked.

"John dated one of the nurses at the Manor House for a while, and neither his father nor his brother approved of the girl for some reason," Mr. Carlino said.

"Why didn't they approve?" Julie asked.

"I didn't eavesdrop that closely," Mr. Carlino said and winked. "Though I tried. From what I heard, they didn't trust her for some reason. John broke up with her under pressure. He was bitter. The girl was bitter too. I heard her talking about it later with the other nurses. It happens all the time, I'm sad to say. My wife's family pressured her to give up on me when I was diagnosed with my disease."

"Her family was against you?" Julie asked.

"They were once it looked like I wasn't going to make big bucks being a rich young doctor," the man in the wheelchair said wistfully. "After a few months, my wife started to see things the same way . . . And so it goes . . ."

"That was really mean," Clarice said.

"I thought so too." Mr. Carlino pushed his wheelchair toward the elevators.

"Can I see the watch?" Clarice asked. Julie handed it to her. Clarice read off the names and dates as she walked down the hallway.

"I wonder why she was so worried about this watch," Clarice said.

"It must have great sentimental value," Julie said.

"But remember how she acted," Rebecca said. "She did seem a bit odd."

"Read the names and dates again," Mr. Carlino said as they reached the elevator.

Clarice read off the Babbage children's names and the birth dates as the elevator went to the second floor.

"Read the date of their wedding again," Joe Carlino said.

"December 10, 1937," Clarice said.

"Read Sarah's birth date again," the man in the wheelchair said.

"Sarah was born on August 10, 1936," Clarice said.

"Sarah was born over a year before Mrs. Babbage was married," Julie said with surprise.

"Sounds like it," Mr. Carlino said. The elevator doors opened. The children looked at each other.

"I think that solves another mystery," Mr. Carlino said.

"You mean she got pregnant and had a baby before she was married?" Clarice thought for a moment. "Well, that's not so strange."

"Out-of-wedlock babies were much more of a scandal back in the thirties than they are today," Mr. Carlino said. "I'm sure she was, and is, embarrassed."

"From the way she talked this morning it sounded like it still bothered her," Julie said softly. "If she still felt ashamed, that would explain why she was so upset."

"If she's really embarrassed, maybe we shouldn't say anything," Clarice replied. "I mean, she's so old, and now she's really sick too."

"I think Clarice is right." Julie was surprised at the sound of her own words. "I think we should keep her secret a secret if that's what she wanted. Real detectives are supposed to keep things confidential."

"I won't say anything," Clarice said.

"Me either," Julie agreed.

"My lips are sealed." Mr. Carlino ran an imaginary zipper across his mouth. The other girls agreed.

They all went down the hall silently, each thinking about Mrs. Babbage. When they entered the intensive care wing, Julie wasn't sure she wanted to see Mrs. Babbage even if they were allowed to.

The intensive care wing smelled very much like a hospital, Julie thought. She didn't really care for the odor of medicine and antiseptic.

"What are you doing here, Mr. Carlino?" a nurse asked as she pushed a cart out of the room. She smiled, popping her chewing gum. The badge on her white dress said *Nancy Waters, R.N.* She was a tall woman with dark brown hair that looked dyed. She was pretty but wore a lot of makeup, Julie thought. Her beauty was harsh, not soft like Julie's mother's face.

"We're looking for Mrs. Babbage's daughter," the man in the wheelchair said.

"Oh, really?" the nurse asked, looking curiously at the children.

"They have something that belongs to her and want to give it to her daughter," Mr. Carlino said. "Do you know how Mrs. Babbage is doing?"

"Between you and me, not good," the nurse said. "I'm not sure she's going to make it through the night. She's in a coma, you know."

"We heard she was in bad shape," Clarice said.

"At least they can't blame this one on me or other innocent people," Nurse Waters said. "I told that state inspector and everyone else that I never did anything wrong. But Ms. Dearborn had to save her own skin. She didn't care about the truth. I guess she's looking hard for some other poor fools to blame this time. I feel sorry for Mr. Binton and Mrs. Babbage though."

"Did you know Mr. Binton?" Julie asked.

"Know him?" she asked. "I dated John Binton for almost a year. Then he dumped me when the accusations about Mrs. Applewhite started to fly. Of course he would have dumped me anyway. Mr. Binton didn't like me."

"You're the one?" Clarice asked. "We were just talking about you."

"Talking about me?" the nurse said slyly. "Mr. Carlino, you always said you didn't repeat gossip."

"But Mr. Carlino didn't mention you by name," Julie said quickly. "We just saw John and Roger Binton down in the morgue and, well, one thing led to another. We heard about you and the other nurses being fired."

"It's okay, honey." Nurse Waters popped her gum. "I'm better off without them. They were a bunch of losers. Rich losers. But money isn't everything. Is it, Mr. Carlino?"

"Not at all," Mr. Carlino said. "And the way things look today, you probably are better off without John Binton."

"What do you mean?" the nurse asked, popping her gum

again. She smiled deliciously. "You've heard something, haven't you? Come on, tell me. We're old pals. Did little Johnny get caught with his hand in the cash register? He hated his father and brother, if you want to know the truth. I mean, he despised them, and I'm not kidding. I dated him for a year, and I should know. He had lots of good ideas for the business, but his father was too old-fashioned to listen, and his brother was afraid to try new ventures. Johnny was weak, really. I am better off without him. That's what I told the police earlier this week. A man named Detective Ortiz was asking me questions a few days ago. You know something, Mr. Carlino. Come on and tell!"

"We shouldn't discuss police business, should we?" Julie asked Mr. Carlino, touching his arm. She thought the nurse was being too nosy and gossipy.

"Julie's probably right," the man in the wheelchair said reluctantly. "I imagine you'll be reading about it in the newspapers soon enough."

"Aw, come on, Joe," the nurse said. "I'd tell you if it was the other way around."

"I know you would." Mr. Carlino chuckled. "Nurse Waters was one of the best sources of news at the Manor House."

"Until they fired me and the others on some false negligent-care charges," the nurse said bitterly. "Luckily Mrs. Pierce got me a job here at the hospital with her. I don't like my hours as well, but it's a lot better than working for Ms. High-and-Mighty-Masters-in-Business-Administration Dearborn. She'll be out on her . . . well, I was going to say something else, but since you church kids are here, I'll spare you the full version. But Mrs. Pierce and

I are going to sue her and the Manor House for defamation of character and for firing us. And after this week's events, I think we're going to have a very good case. We'll be rolling in settlement money, and Ms. High-and-Mighty will be on the sidewalk wondering what happened. Let her feel what it's like to get fired."

"We'd better find Mrs. Babbage's daughter," Julie said. Nurse Waters looked as if she was just getting her second wind.

"She's down in the waiting room." The nurse popped her gum. "She's the one with the red blouse."

"We'd better be on our way," Mr. Carlino said softly.

"I've got my rounds to make too," Nurse Waters said more calmly. "I'd like to talk to you later, if you've got time."

"We'll see," Mr. Carlino said.

Nurse Waters pushed her cart down the hallway. As she left, a pack of chewing gum fell off the cart. Clarice rushed forward. She bent down to pick up the gum. She started to call out to give it back to her, but hesitated. Nurse Waters pushed her cart into the next room and shut the door behind her.

Chapter Nine

Nurse Waters's Missing Gum

"What's wrong?" Julie asked Clarice.

"That nurse dropped her gum." Clarice had a puzzled expression on her face.

"Why didn't you give it to her?" Julie asked.

"I don't know," Clarice said. "I was trying to think of something. Then she went into that room."

There was a sign on the door that said only authorized people were supposed to go inside.

"You can give it to her later," Julie said. "Or leave it at the nurses' station. Let's give back the watch and get out of here. I'm tired of being around all these sick, unhappy people." Julie walked quickly down the hall toward the waiting room.

"What's the matter with her?" Clarice asked. "I didn't mean to make her mad."

"I think she's just upset," Emily said with concern.

"She's been acting a little weird all day."

"I've had days like that." Clarice nodded. "We should be extra nice to her."

Rebecca and Emily looked at each other. Emily grinned slightly. The two girls almost began to giggle.

"What are you smiling about?" Clarice asked.

"Nothing," Emily said. "We were just agreeing with you that we should be extra nice to Julie."

"I agree." Emily forced herself not to smile.

The three girls ran to catch up with Julie and Mr. Carlino. They all reached the door to the intensive care waiting room at the same time.

"That must be her." Julie pointed to a woman sitting on a couch reading a magazine. She wore a red blouse.

"Are you Mrs. Babbage's daughter?" Julie asked.

"I'm Sarah Babbage O'Conner." The woman stood up.

"We have something for you." Julie and the others quickly introduced themselves. Then Julie began telling the story about the missing watch.

"So we finally found the watch in Mr. Binton's things," Julie said. "And we brought it up here to you because we knew your mom thought it was really important."

Mrs. Babbage's oldest daughter took the watch carefully. She wiped a tear out of her eye.

"Actually, my mother hated this watch." She sniffed. Clarice quickly grabbed a tissue from a box on the couch and handed it to the teary woman. "She and my father used to argue about it. She called me early this morning because she was upset that it was lost. I'm surprised she didn't throw it away once he died. But she loved my father. And she loved my sisters and me. She has been a very good mother to us all. And my dad was a very wonderful man. I couldn't have asked for a better father. He passed away three years ago . . . There's a lot of history in this watch."

Mrs. Babbage's daughter teared up again. Clarice handed her another tissue. The woman mouthed a silent thank-you. Julie began to feel uneasy, watching the woman cry.

"Did my mother tell you why she was so anxious to get this watch back?" the woman asked Julie.

"I'm sure it was because she loved your father," Clarice said quickly.

"Well, love is all that matters in the end," Mrs. Babbage's daughter said softly, looking down at the worn timepiece. She rubbed the metal with her thumb.

"We'd better go now," Julie said.

"I'm sure my mother will be glad that you found it," the woman said.

"I'm glad too," Julie said gently. "Your mom is really nice, and we're really sorry that she's so sick."

The woman nodded. She sniffled again and blew her nose. She put the watch in her purse.

"I was just getting ready to go in and see her again," the woman said. "I'll be sure to give it to her when she wakes up." Sarah Babbage O'Conner walked across the room. Her shoes squeaked. She looked over her shoulder.

"I just bought these shoes," the woman said self-consciously. "They squeak so much I'm going to take them back."

Julie nodded. She took a deep breath. Clarice stared at the floor, as if listening or looking for something.

"Let's get out of here," Julie said. "We solved the mystery

of the missing watch. I'm ready to go home."

The children filed silently out of the room and walked to the elevator.

"You guys go on," Clarice said slowly. "I want to give the gum back to that nurse."

"Okay," Julie said. "We'll wait downstairs. But don't be too long."

The three children and the man in the wheelchair got into the elevator. They rode down to the ground floor without speaking. The bell dinged, and the doors whooshed open.

The girls walked to the lobby and sat down in chairs to wait. Mr. Carlino rolled up next to Julie.

"I'm glad you ladies had the maturity to keep Mrs. Babbage's secret," Joe Carlino said.

"It's kind of sad, if she's been worried about that since 1937," Rebecca mused. "That's a long time to worry about something."

"I hope Clarice doesn't take too long," Julie said impatiently. "Maybe we should go back and get her. We could be here all day if she gets lost or something. It's almost three o'clock. They are probably done with the crafts at the nursing home."

"Maybe you should go get her," Rebecca suggested.

"Give her a few more minutes," Emily said. "How long does it take to give someone a pack of gum? I want to go back too, but she is trying to do something kind."

"We can wait a few more minutes, I guess." Julie looked at her watch and then at the elevators. She started tapping her toe.

* * *

Upstairs in the intensive care wing, Clarice waited several minutes in the hall. She was sure Nurse Waters would come out of one of the rooms any moment. Finally she went to the nurses' station. She was just about to ask where to find her when Nurse Waters came out of a doorway at the end of the hall. She rolled her cart down the hall. Clarice walked softly up behind the nurse and followed her for several steps. Nurse Waters was looking down at her chart when Clarice finally tapped her on the shoulder.

"Whoa!" Nurse Waters jerked and whirled around. "Honey, you shouldn't sneak up on a person like that."

"I'm sorry," Clarice said. "You dropped your gum when you were at the Manor House today, and I forgot to give it to you earlier."

"Thank you, sweetheart." The nurse took the gum quickly, and then she frowned. She stared at the girl and smiled. "But you must be mistaken. I don't work at the Manor House anymore."

"I know that," Clarice said. "But I saw you today in the hallway, remember? I was praying with Aunt Esther and I looked up and saw you. I heard your shoes making that squishy sound as you walked by."

"Oh . . ." The large woman looked unsettled.

"And then you took your cart into Mrs. Babbage's room, and then you went down to Mrs. Barclay's room," Clarice said. "She saw you too. In fact, when I asked her who came in her room, she identified you."

"Mrs. Barclay is as crazy as a loon, honey," Nurse Waters said.

"Everyone thinks so," Clarice replied. "But Aunt Esther

told me that one thing old people really need is someone to listen to them. Just listen. So I listened. And when I asked her who came into her room, she said, 'Waters.'"

"She did?" The nurse looked down the hall uncomfortably.

"Yes," Clarice said. "Everyone thought she was asking for water, but she didn't want a drink. She was answering our question. She isn't crazy all the time. She recognized you. And I think there's a lot more going on than that. I think you had a motive to kill Mr. Binton and blame his sons and also blame Ms. Dearborn. In fact, I bet you've been planning this whole thing ever since you got fired."

"Well, you are right about my being at the nursing home today," Nurse Waters said. Then she began whispering. "But the rest of your story is all wrong. I'm on a team investigating the Manor House for the police and state board. Ms. Dearborn doesn't know anything about it, of course. But we think she's the murderer."

"What?" Clarice asked, confused. She looked suspiciously at the large nurse. "I don't believe that."

"Sure, I can tell you all about it," Nurse Waters said. "That lady is bad news. She is trying to frame the Bintons, not me. Listen. My feet are killing me because these new shoes are too tight. That's why they squeak. Let's go sit down and have a soda, and I'll tell you all about my investigation. We can get to the lunchroom this way."

"I don't know . . ." Clarice said with a frown.

The tall nurse opened a door at the end of the hall. Clarice started to jerk back to run. Just then, she saw the steel flash of a large hypodermic needle in Nurse Waters's hand. The nurse grabbed Clarice's arm and yanked at the same time, pulling Clarice through the door.

Her muscular arm pressed down hard on Clarice's windpipe. With the other hand she pressed the tip of the needle against Clarice's neck.

"You scream or give me any trouble, kid, and I will stick you good. I've got enough morphine in this needle to make you go to sleep permanently. Do you hear me, kid?"

Clarice moaned, nodding her head up and down. The tall nurse dragged Clarice farther into the dark room.

Chapter Ten

The Angel's Watchful Eye

The elevator doors swished open, and Julie walked out quickly onto the second floor.

"I knew we shouldn't have left Clarice," she said to Mr. Carlino as he rolled his wheelchair out into the hallway. Rebecca and Emily had decided to wait downstairs in the lobby. "I bet she got lost."

Julie peered up and down the hall. She didn't see anyone familiar.

"We can check down by the intensive care waiting room," Mr. Carlino said. Julie followed him, but the waiting room was empty.

Julie walked up to the nurses' station. A woman sat behind the desk, typing on a keyboard in front of a computer.

"Can you tell me where Nurse Waters would be?" Julie asked.

The woman looked down at a chart. "She should be making her rounds in 222 through 228."

"Which way is that?"

"It's down at the end of the hall to your right. The rooms on the left are part of the new wing and are unoccupied."

"Thanks."

"She could also be on her break," the woman called out. "She might be getting a soda at the machine down at room 210."

"I'll check the soda machine," Mr. Carlino said.

"I'll check the other rooms," Julie said.

Julie's eyes brightened when she saw the nurse's cart at the far end of the hallway. But when she knocked on the door of room 228, no one answered. She peeked in. A man was lying in the bed in the darkened room hooked up to monitors and tubes. Julie checked the next room and the next and the next. All had patients, but there was no sign of Clarice or Nurse Waters.

She stared at the nurse's cart by the last door on the left. She walked over. A sign on the door said *The Gillworst Memorial Foundation Wing*.

She opened the door. She was surprised at the wide-open space before her. A large, shadowy room was divided with rows and rows of vertical metal wall studs. Huge piles of sheetrock and black paint buckets were stacked on the dusty cement floor. Orange electrical cords snaked out across the floor in all directions. Something about the room looked vaguely familiar. She was about to close the door when she heard a faint noise in the distance.

"Clarice?" Julie called out. "Nurse Waters?"

Julie was about to walk out, but she couldn't. She felt

something tugging at her, drawing her into the room. She looked down. She saw the shiny foil of a pack of gum on the floor just inside the room. She picked it up. It looked like the same type of gum Clarice had had earlier. Julie held the gum.

She pulled the cart into the doorway. Then she let go of the door, which only closed part way because the cart blocked it from shutting. The extra light from the hallway was comforting.

The room was dark but not too dark to see. Far on the other side of the huge room, a beam of light shone down from the ceiling. Julie walked carefully and slowly toward the light, making her way past the piles of sheetrock and lumber.

"Clarice!" Julie called out. "Are you in here? Nurse Waters?"

The silence of the huge room was beginning to feel eerie. A large unpainted wall, dividing the area in half, blocked her vision. Julie found a pathway through all the construction materials. It looked like a future hallway.

She passed beyond the long dividing wall. The beam of light came from a skylight about thirty yards away. Julie walked toward the light.

"Clarice!" She passed a huge pile of sheetrock. The beam of light from the ceiling shone down on a big round circle that was made out of rocks. Julie blinked. A tarp covered something in the center of the circle. The big round circle seemed oddly out of place. She walked toward it for a better look.

Once she got closer, she realized she was looking at a stone fountain. A platform was in the center of the fountain, with the tarp covering something tall. The bottom of the pool was filled with dark, stagnant water. Julie crinkled her nose because there was a dank, sour smell.

The water moved around the fountain. Julie frowned. She couldn't understand why the water was moving.

Then she saw a tiny trickle of water running out from underneath the tarp. Julie leaned over and lifted up the edge of the tarp. She saw the tip of a white marble wing that looked as if it belonged to a large bird.

She stepped back, taking a deep breath. She lifted the tarp higher and saw that there were the legs of a man behind the wing. She pulled the tarp all the way off. She was looking at the back of the statue of an angel poised to take flight. A bright orange electrical cord was wrapped around the angel's back.

Julie walked slowly around to the front of the statue, her eyes following the stripe of orange cord. She gasped in disbelief when she saw the cord wrapped around Clarice, who was tied tightly, pressed between the angel's big marble arms. Clarice's eyes and mouth were covered with white surgical tape. Her hands were hidden behind her back. Her pale cheeks were streaked with tears.

"Clarice, what are you doing up there?" Then Julie suddenly remembered her dream. The large room under construction, a pool of water, angels watching. From the corner of her eye she saw a movement of white and a flash of steel as a voice screamed out like an angry tiger.

Julie instinctively ducked, just as she did in her dream, as the arm came down, holding the long sharp needle.

Nurse Waters lost her balance when Julie ducked. She tried to correct her swing, but that threw her off balance.

She swung beyond Julie and toppled forward over Julie's back. The weight of her body smashed Julie into the side of the fountain, but the tall woman kept going. Her head bent down and her feet flipped all the way over in a huge somersault. She landed on her back, partway in the water, her feet slamming into the angel in the center of the fountain. The dank water splashed up over the walls of the fountain.

Then everything was quiet, except Clarice, who was wiggling and moaning. She was soaking wet from the splash caused by the tall nurse.

"Help! Help!" Julie screamed. "We're in here! Help us, please! Help!"

Julie jumped over the fountain wall. She pulled the tape off Clarice's eyes first. Clarice blinked in terror. She tossed her head back and forth.

"It's okay. It's me, Clarice." Julie looked at Nurse Waters. The tall woman was not moving. Julie's hands trembled wildly as she began to loosen the thick electrical cord from around Clarice. Once the cord was loose, she pulled it totally off. Clarice jumped into the water and over the fountain wall.

Clarice pulled the tape off her mouth by herself as Julie climbed quickly out of the smelly, dark water. The nurse moaned, moving slightly.

Julie looked down at Nurse Waters. The back of her head was wedged against the inner wall of the fountain. Her lips and mouth were just above the water. The rest of her torso was lying in the dark water until her legs rose up and rested on the base of the statue. The shiny stainless steel syringe was lying on the fountain's edge.

"Are you okay?" Julie asked Clarice.

"She tied me up," Clarice said. "And she threatened to stick me with the needle if I didn't do what she said."

"We need to get help." Julie was breathless. "Help! Somebody, help!" She yelled as loudly as she could. She thought she heard voices in the distance.

Clarice looked down at the tall woman. She felt frozen. All she could do was stare back and forth from the motionless woman in the water to the shiny needle on the fountain's edge.

Suddenly lights went on in the big room.

"Over here by the fountain!" Julie yelled. The sound of rapid footsteps was followed by the appearance of running workmen.

"She's dangerous!" Clarice pointed at the woman in the water. "She tried to hurt me."

More people rushed into the room, including Sergeant Haskins and some other policemen.

"She tied up Clarice and threatened her with that!" Julie pointed to the needle. The tall nurse was waking up. "She may have even stuck herself accidentally. She might be poisoned."

Sergeant Haskins nodded seriously. He barked out orders to the other officers.

Julie smiled when she saw Mr. Carlino rolling his wheelchair through the unfinished room. He looked relieved when he saw Julie and Clarice. Julie waved.

"Let's get out of here." Julie wiped a strand of wet red hair from Clarice's face. Julie took Clarice by the hand and began leading her out.

Chapter Eleven

The Father's Loving Care

The next Saturday, the four girls gathered at the Manor House to help with crafts. The big recreation room was filled with old and young people, carefully quilting, knitting, doing needlecraft and making all sorts of other handcrafts.

In one corner of the room, Julie and her friends were sitting next to Mr. Carlino, who had rolled his wheelchair up to the table. Mrs. Babbage, who had returned from the hospital on Thursday, sat at another table helping Clarice. A few feet away, old Aunt Esther sat near the large windows that faced out onto the green courtyard. She looked at the children and smiled, while her hands worked busily on the knitting that rested in her lap.

Mrs. Babbage was still a bit pale, but her face was relaxed and content. She helped Clarice put a brightly colored thread through the eye of a needle. Seeing Mrs.

Babbage's face at rest filled Julie's heart with a sudden gust of compassion. For a moment her eyes welled up with tears as she watched the old woman.

"You girls really made a difference in Mrs. Babbage's life." Joe Carlino watched the older woman help the young girl. "She's like a new person."

"Renewed, is what God would say," Julie replied. "Only God can make sick people well, but he can also make old things new, and wrong things right, and cause all things to work together for good because of his loving care for us. That's what my father says all the time. With someone like Mrs. Babbage, you can really see a change. Look how peaceful she looks."

"Letting go of painful secrets will do that," Mr. Carlino said. "Practically everyone in the whole Manor House has remarked about the change they see in her. People were surprised when she told them the story of her oldest daughter, but no one was unkind. In fact, Mrs. Babbage shared the whole thing at dinner the first night she got back. Her oldest daughter was with her and helped her talk about it."

"Sarah didn't even know her biological father, did she?" Rebecca asked.

"No," Emily said. "Sarah's father and Mrs. Babbage planned to be married. Then he died on the eve of their wedding in a car wreck. But she was pregnant. So when Sarah was born, her biological father was long gone. But by then Mr. Babbage had proposed. He must have been a brave man and a loving, caring father. He adopted Sarah, and they had the three other girls."

"I'm glad she was able to talk about it with her friends,"

Julie said. "Mrs. Babbage said Aunt Esther visited her at the hospital last week and talked with her. After praying with Aunt Esther, Mrs. Babbage said she could feel God's forgiveness. Can you imagine living with something like that for so long and always feeling guilty?"

"That's more years than all of us have lived combined," Rebecca asked. "Except for Mr. Carlino."

"I didn't think she would say anything publicly," Mr. Carlino said. "But one of the first people she told was Mrs. Gillworst. Now it's had a ripple effect. Last night a number of the ladies were sharing old secrets around the dinner table. Even Mrs. Gillworst had a few confessions to make. I've never seen them so lively."

"My mom says that it was a real scandal back then to have illegitimate children," Rebecca said.

"A whole lot more than it is now." Mr. Carlino nodded.

"It made me think of Mary and Jesus," Rebecca said. "Remember that sermon your father gave last Christmas? He said that Mary had to fight shame because she was pregnant before she was married, and no one really knew it was Jesus, the Son of God. It must have been hard for her and Joseph and their families to hear people whispering and talking about them."

"Yeah, I never thought of it quite that way," Emily said.

"I wish Nurse Waters had gotten over her problems," Julie said. "She would have saved herself and everyone a lot of pain. We went to Mr. Binton's funeral, and his family was so upset."

"The police are charging Nurse Waters with murder and three counts of attempted murder," Mr. Carlino replied. "The police say she gave a full confession. You and Clarice are sure lucky to be alive."

"God was watching out for us." Julie carefully cut a patch of cloth for her quilt. "I don't know if I've ever been so scared in my life. I hate needles. But it seemed as if God was right there watching over me, just like that statue of the angel. I remembered my dream just in time, and I ducked automatically as she came at me, as if I were following the script of a movie. The whole thing was so strange."

"I hope she gets what she deserves," Rebecca said.

"The police have a strong case," Mr. Carlino said. "Being rejected by John Binton and losing her job was just too much for her to handle. She was so angry she wanted those who hurt her to suffer. She was able to act controlled on the outside, but she was really unbalanced."

"She panicked when Clarice confronted her," Julie said. "She tied her up, trying to buy time and think of a way to escape."

"I would have been scared to death with someone holding a needle to my neck like that," Emily said. "Clarice is braver than I thought."

"She was mad at herself later," Julie said. "You should have heard her in the hallway at the hospital. She said she knew Nurse Waters was lying, but she couldn't think of anything to say fast enough. And by the time she decided to run away, Nurse Waters was just a split second faster. And really strong."

"Well, Clarice was still brave," Mr. Carlino said. "And so were you, Julie."

"Yeah," Emily said.

"It sure helped that she stuck herself with some of that morphine," Julie said. "It made her groggy. I was scared she'd wake up before I got Clarice untied and out of there."

"She got a taste of her own medicine, as we used to say when I was a kid," Mr. Carlino said.

"I feel sorry for the Bintons," Julie said. "Her plan almost worked. John Binton really looked guilty. Sergeant Haskins said Nurse Waters planted the insulin bottles and syringes in his car trunk too. She was really thorough."

"She also made Ms. Dearborn look really bad, as if she were trying to cover up negligence," Mr. Carlino said.

"But why would she go after Mrs. Babbage too?" Rebecca asked. "She could already frame John Binton and make the Manor House look negligent by giving Mr. Binton the wrong medicine."

"The police said Nurse Waters thought Mr. Binton might have told Mrs. Babbage something incriminating before he died," Mr. Carlino replied. "He and Mrs. Babbage were friends, and they were talking that evening, plus she was the only one there to hear his dying words. But it was more than that fear. She didn't like Mrs. Babbage anyway, since Mrs. Babbage had complained about her when Mrs. Applewhite died. Nurse Waters wanted to make sure no one caused her problems. She wanted to be thorough. She is obviously a very disturbed and dangerous woman. I knew she was upset, but I had no idea that she was eaten up with such anger and bitterness."

"Well, that's the way I was," Julie said thoughtfully.

"What do you mean?" Mr. Carlino looked surprised.

"I was very upset with Clarice the morning we came to the Manor House to help Mrs. Babbage find her watch. Clarice was acting so snotty, and I resented her so much that I just about came unglued myself. I was bitter and angry.

Everybody wanted me to be nice to her, and I just couldn't stand it."

"I do remember you had a little outburst about her after they took Mrs. Babbage to the hospital," the man in the wheelchair recalled.

"Little outburst?" Julie said in surprise. "I really lost it. But Clarice and I have patched things up. I asked her to forgive me, and she did the same. An amazing change has come over her. And maybe I've changed too."

"It shows real strength of character when people are able to admit wrong and change their ways. You are more than a good detective, Julie," Mr. Carlino said, "you're a person who has something special inside."

Julie smiled at the compliment. "Well, I think it is more that there is *someone* special inside. But I can see that you haven't lost your touch. You're still good at making people feel good," she said with a giggle. "That's why Ms. Dearborn hired you to manage the nursing staff. She finally began to appreciate your people skills, I guess."

"We'll see how it works out," the man in the wheelchair said. "I do feel good about working again. Even though it's not the same as a medical practice, it's still in the medical field. And having more money is a big help. I'm still not letting them call me doctor. Not unless they pay me like a doctor to hear people's complaints."

"It's almost time to pray with Aunt Esther." Julie looked at her watch. "She promised she would pray with Clarice and the rest of us today."

Julie walked over to get Clarice. She waited because Clarice was preoccupied.

"Now you're getting it," Mrs. Babbage said approvingly

to Clarice.

"Thank you." Clarice had never done any needlework, but she was determined to try. She had spent a long time at the craft store picking out a pattern. She had finally chosen the pattern of a large angel that resembled the statue in the fountain. She had already told Julie that her plan was to give the completed needlework to her.

"I think it will look good," Julie said, as Clarice pulled the long thread through the thick material at the tip of the angel's wing.

"It looks a lot like that angel, doesn't it?" Clarice asked.

"Yes, Clarice," Julie said. "It's lovely."

"Good." Clarice pulled the thread through again. "I think it will look great on your wall."

"I never thought you would want to do needlepoint," Julie said.

"Me either," Clarice said. "But it makes it different when you're doing it for someone else and not just filling up time. This needlepoint has a purpose. It's a present, but I want it to be a reminder of your saving my life."

"It reminds me of the power of prayer too," Rebecca said. "I've been waiting all week for Aunt Esther to tell us how she knows things."

"Me too," Julie said. "It's almost time for us to pray. My mom said we could stay late, Aunt Esther."

The old woman was walking slowly over to the girls. She smiled, showing her ancient yellow teeth and gold fillings.

"All of God's children can pray," Aunt Esther said firmly. "And we are the Father's children. My mother taught me to pray when I was just around your age. And I was thirteen when God started to give me a concern about

China. I read about the Chinese in our local newspaper. And that night I began to pray. Of course I never thought I'd actually go to China. That was too much for a little girl on a farm to even consider. But God has his ways. Watch and pray, the Father says, watch and pray."

The girls gathered in the corner of the Recreation Room. The old woman smiled and began helping them to pray. At first it was a little awkward. But suddenly, it was like a fresh breeze blowing through a flower garden. Julie could feel the words rising up out of her heart, as if being pulled along like the wind pulls a kite . . .

Also by John Bibee

THE SPIRIT FLYER SERIES

During the course of a year, the ordinary town of Centerville becomes the setting for some extraordinary events. When several children discover that Spirit Flyer bicycles possess strange and wondrous powers, they are thrust into a conflict with Goliath Industries—with the fate of the town in the balance.

Book 1 *The Magic Bicycle*
Book 2 *The Toy Campaign*
Book 3 *The Only Game in Town*
Book 4 *Bicycle Hills*
Book 5 *The Last Christmas*
Book 6 *The Runaway Parents*
Book 7 *The Perfect Star*
Book 8 *The Journey of Wishes*